"Here he is at **to present you to my cousin Idris, Sheikh of Zahrat."**

Arden widened her smile, determined not to be overawed by meeting her very first, and no doubt last, sheikh. Coming to this formal reception, surrounded by VIPs who oozed money and privilege, had already tested her nerves.

She turned, tilted her head to look up and felt the world drop away.

His face was severely sculpted as if scored by desert winds. Yet there was beauty in those high cheekbones and his firm yet sensual mouth. His nose and jaw were honed and strong. The harsh angle of those beetling black brows intimidated. So did the wide flare of his nostrils, as if the sheikh scented something unexpected.

Shock dragged at her, loosening her knees till her legs felt like rubber.

His eyes...

Dark as a midnight storm, those eyes fixed on her instinctive movement as she clutched Hamid for support. Slowly they lifted again to clash with hers, disdain clear in that haughty stare.

A shuddering wave of disquiet rolled through her as she blinked up, telling herself it wasn't possible. It couldn't be.

Despite the frantic messages her body was sending her, she *couldn't* know this man.

Yet her brain wouldn't listen to reason. It told her it was *him*. The man who'd changed her life.

Secret Heirs of Billionaires

There are some things money can't buy...

Living life at lightning pace, these magnates are no strangers to stakes at their highest. It seems they've got it all... That is, until they find out that there's an unplanned item to add to their list of accomplishments!

Achieved:

1. Successful business empire

2. Beautiful women in their bed

3. *An heir to bear their name...?*

Though every billionaire needs to leave his legacy in safe hands, discovering a secret heir shakes up his carefully orchestrated plan in more ways than one!

Uncover their secrets in:

Unwrapping the Castelli Secret by Caitlin Crews

Brunetti's Secret Son by Maya Blake

The Secret to Marrying Marchesi by Amanda Cinelli

Demetriou Demands His Child by Kate Hewitt

Look out for more stories in
the **Secret Heirs of Billionaires** series
coming soon!

Annie West

THE DESERT KING'S SECRET HEIR

CANCELLED

HARLEQUIN PRESENTS®

Recycling programs
for this product may
not exist in your area.

ISBN-13: 978-0-373-13970-5

The Desert King's Secret Heir

First North American Publication 2016

Copyright © 2016 by Annie West

Printed in U.S.A.

www.Harlequin.com

Growing up near the beach, **Annie West** spent lots of time observing tall, burnished lifeguards—early research! Now she spends her days fantasizing about gorgeous men and their love lives. Annie has been a reader all her life. She also loves travel, long walks, good company and great food. You can contact her at annie@annie-west.com or via PO Box 1041, Warners Bay, NSW 2282, Australia.

Books by Annie West

Harlequin Presents

The Flaw in Raffaele's Revenge
Seducing His Enemy's Daughter
Damaso Claims His Heir
Imprisoned by a Vow
Captive in the Spotlight
Defying Her Desert Duty
Prince of Scandal

One Night With Consequences
A Vow to Secure His Legacy

Seven Sexy Sins
The Sinner's Marriage Redemption

Desert Vows
The Sheikh's Princess Bride
The Sultan's Harem Bride

At His Service
An Enticing Debt to Pay

Dark-Hearted Tycoons
Undone by His Touch

Sinful Desert Nights
Girl in the Bedouin Tent

Visit the Author Profile page at Harlequin.com for more titles.

This book is dedicated to the wonderful men
in my family across three generations:
all heroic in their own way.

What excellent role models for my heroes!

CHAPTER ONE

'LET ME BE the first to congratulate you, Cousin. May you and your Princess be happy all your days.'

Hamid beamed with such goodwill Idris felt his own mouth kick up in a rare smile. They might not be close but Idris had missed his older cousin as they'd carved separate lives for themselves, Idris in Zahrat and Hamid as a UK-based academic.

'Not my Princess yet, Hamid.' He kept his voice soft, aware that, despite the chatter of a few hundred VIPs, there were plenty of ears eager for news of his impending nuptials.

Hamid's eyes widened behind rimless glasses. 'Have I put my foot in it? I'd heard—'

'You heard correctly.' Idris paused, tugging in a breath before it lengthened into a sigh. He had to conquer this sense of constraint whenever he thought of his upcoming marriage.

No one forced his hand. He was Sheikh Idris Baddour, supreme ruler of Zahrat, protector of the weak, defender of his nation. His word was law in his own country and, for that matter, here in his opulent London embassy.

Yet he hadn't chosen marriage. It had chosen him—a necessary arrangement. To cement stability in his region. To ensure the line of succession. To prove that, despite his modern reformist ways, he respected the traditions of his people. So much rode on his wedding.

Change had been hard won in Zahrat. A willingness to conform in the matter of a suitable, dynastically necessary marriage would win over the last of the old guard who'd fretted over his reforms. They'd viewed him as an unseasoned pup when he'd taken over at just twenty-six. After four years they knew better. But there was no escaping the fact this wedding would achieve what strong leadership and diplomacy hadn't.

'It's not official yet,' he murmured to Hamid. 'You know how slowly such negotiations proceed.'

'You're a lucky man. Princess Ghizlan is beautiful and intelligent. She'll make you a perfect wife.'

Idris glanced to the woman holding court nearby. Resplendent in a blood-red evening gown that clung to a perfect hourglass figure, she was the stuff of male fantasy. Add her bred-in-the-bone understanding of Middle Eastern politics and her charming yet assured manner and he knew he was a lucky man.

Pity he didn't feel like one.

Even the thought of acquainting himself with that lush body didn't excite him.

What did that say about his libido?

Too many hours brokering peace negotiations with not one but two difficult neighbouring countries. Too many evenings strategising to push reform in a nation still catching up with the twenty-first century.

And before that too many shallow sexual encounters with women who were accommodating but unimportant.

'Thank you, Hamid. I'm sure she will.' As the daughter of a neighbouring ruler and a means to ensure long-term peace, Ghizlan would be invaluable. As the prospective mother of a brood of children she'd be priceless. Those children would ensure his sheikhdom wasn't racked by the disruption it had faced when his uncle died without a son.

Idris told himself his lack of enthusiasm would evaporate once he and Ghizlan shared a bed. He tried to picture her there, her ebony hair spread on the pillow. But to his chagrin his mind inserted an image of hair the colour of a sunburst. Of curling locks soft as down.

'You'll have to come home for the ceremony. It will be good to have you there for a while instead of buried in this cold, grey place.'

Hamid smiled. 'You're biased. There's much to be said for England.'

'Of course there is. It's an admirable country.'

Idris glanced around, reminding himself they might be overheard.

Hamid's smile became a chuckle. 'It's got a lot going for it.' He leaned even closer, his voice dropping further. 'Including a very special woman. Someone I want you to meet.'

Idris felt his eyes widen. Hamid with a serious girlfriend? 'She must be out of the ordinary.'

One thing the men in his family excelled at was avoiding commitment to women. He'd been a case in point until political necessity forced his hand. His father had been famous for sowing his wild oats, even after marriage. And their uncle, the previous Sheikh, had been too busy enjoying the charms of his mistresses to father a child with his long-suffering spouse.

'She is. Enough to make me rethink my life.'

'Another academic?'

'Nothing so dull.'

Idris stared. Hamid lived for his research. That was why he'd been passed over for the throne when their uncle died. Everyone, Hamid included, acknowledged he was too absorbed in history to excel at running a nation.

'Will I meet this paragon tonight?'

Hamid nodded, his eyes alight. 'She's just gone to freshen up before—ah, there she is.' He gestured to the far end of the room. 'Isn't she lovely?'

Only a man besotted would expect him to identify an unknown woman in that crowd. Idris followed Hamid's eager gaze. Was it the tall brunette in black? The svelte blonde in beads and diamonds? Surely not the woman with the braying laugh and the oversized rings flashing like beacons beneath the chandelier?

The crowd shifted and he caught a sliver of silk in softest green, skin as pale as milk and hair that shone like the sky at dawn, rose and gold together.

His pulse thudded once, hard enough to stall his breath. Low in his belly an unfamiliar sensation eddied. A sensation that made his nape prickle.

Then his view was blocked by a couple of men in dinner jackets.

'Which one is she?' His voice echoed strangely, no doubt due to the acoustics of the filled-to-capacity ballroom.

For a second he'd experienced something he hadn't felt in years. A tug of attraction so strong he'd convinced himself it hadn't been real, that imagination had turned a brief interlude into something almost…significant. No doubt because of the dark, relentlessly tough days that had followed. She'd been the one lover he'd had to put aside before his passion was spent. That explained the illusion she was different from the rest.

But the woman he'd known had had a cloud of vibrant curls, not that sleek, conformist chignon.

'I can't see her now. I'll go and fetch her. Unless—' Hamid's smile turned conspiratorial '—you'd like a break from the formalities.'

Tradition decreed that the ruler received his guests on the raised royal dais, complete with a gilded, velvet-cushioned throne for formal audiences. Idris was about to say he'd wait here when something made him pause. How long since he'd allowed himself the luxury of doing something he wanted, not because it was his duty?

Idris's eyes flicked to Ghizlan, easily holding her own with a minor royal and some politicians. As if sensing his regard she looked up, smiled slightly then turned back to her companions.

No doubt about it, she'd make a suitable queen— capable and helpful. Not clinging or needy. Not demanding his attention as too many ex-lovers had done.

Idris turned to Hamid. 'Lead on, Cousin. I'm agog to meet this woman who's captured your heart.'

They wove through the crowd till Hamid halted beside the woman in green. The woman with creamy skin and strawberry-blonde hair and a supple, delicate figure. Idris's attention caught on the lustre of her dress, clinging to her hips and pert bottom.

He stilled, struck by a sensation of déjà vu so strong it eclipsed all else. She said something to his cousin in a soft, lilting voice.

A voice Idris knew.

He frowned, watching Hamid bend his head towards her, seeing her turn a little more so she was in profile.

The conversations around them became white noise, a buzz like swarming insects.

His vision telescoped.

Her lush lips.

Her neat nose.

Her slender, delicate throat.

Two facts hammered into his brain. He knew her, remembered her better than any of the multitude of women who'd once paraded in and out of his life.

And that strange feeling surging up from his gullet and choking his throat with bile was more than surprise or disbelief at the coincidence of meeting her again.

It was fury at the idea she belonged to Hamid.

'Here he is at last. Arden, I'd like to present you to my cousin Idris, Sheikh of Zahrat.'

Arden widened her smile, determined not to be overawed by meeting her very first and no doubt last sheikh. Coming to this formal reception, surrounded by VIPs who oozed money and privilege, had already tested her nerves.

She turned, tilting her head to look up, and felt the world drop away.

His face was severely sculpted as if scored by desert winds. Yet there was beauty in those high cheekbones and his firm yet sensual mouth. His nose and jaw were honed and strong. The harsh angle of those beetling black brows intimidated. So did the wide flare of his nostrils, as if the Sheikh scented something unexpected.

Shock dragged at her, loosening her knees till her legs felt like rubber.

His eyes...

Dark as a midnight storm, those eyes fixed on her instinctive movement as she clutched at Hamid for support. Slowly they lifted again to clash with hers, disdain clear in that haughty stare.

A shuddering wave of disquiet rolled through her as she blinked up, telling herself it wasn't possible. It couldn't be.

Despite the frantic messages her body was sending her, she *couldn't* know this man.

Yet her brain wouldn't listen to reason. It told her it was *him*. The man who'd changed her life.

Heat seared from scalp to toe. Then just as quickly it vanished, leaving her so cold she wouldn't be surprised to hear the crackle of ice forming along her bones, weighing her down.

Her grip on Hamid's arm grew desperate as tiny spots formed and blurred before her eyes. She felt as if she'd slipped out of the real world and into an alternate reality. One where dreams did come true, but so distorted as to be almost unrecognisable.

It wasn't him. It couldn't be. Yet her gaze dropped to his collarbone. Did he have a scar there?

Of course he didn't. This man was tougher, far more daunting than Shakil. She'd bet he didn't do easy, charming smiles. Instead he wore royal authority like a cloak.

Yet she could almost hear herself asking, *Excuse me, Your Highness, would you mind undoing that exquisitely tailored suit and tie so I can check if you have a scar from a riding accident?*

'Arden, are you okay?' Hamid's voice was concerned, his hand warm as it closed over hers.

His touch jerked her back to reality. She slipped her hand from his arm and locked her wobbly knees.

Tonight had revealed, to her astonishment, that Hamid now thought of himself as more than a friend. She couldn't let him labour under that illusion, no matter how grateful she was to him.

'I'm...' She cleared her throat, hesitating. What could she say? *I'm reeling with shock?* 'I'll be all right.'

Yet her gaze clung to that of the man towering before her as if he was some sort of miracle.

It was that realisation that snapped her back to reality. He wasn't Shakil. If he *had* been Shakil, he'd be no miracle, just another of life's tough lessons. A man who'd used her and tossed her aside.

'It's a pleasure to meet you, Your Highness.' Her voice sounded wispy but she persevered. 'I hope you're enjoying your stay in London.'

Belatedly she wondered if she was supposed to

curtsey. Had she offended him? His flesh looked drawn too tight and she glimpsed the rigid line of a tendon standing proud in his neck. He looked ready for battle, not a society meet and greet.

For long seconds silence stretched, as if he didn't want to acknowledge her. She felt her eyebrows pucker into a frown. Beside her Hamid's head swung sharply towards the Sheikh.

'Welcome to my embassy, Ms…'

That voice. He had the same voice.

'Wills, Arden Wills.' Hamid spoke since Arden's voice had disappeared, sucked away by the tidal wave of horror that seized her lungs and stopped her breath.

'Ms Wills.' The Sheikh paused and she glimpsed what almost looked like confusion in those dark eyes, as if he wasn't used to pronouncing such a commonplace name.

But Arden was too busy grappling with her own response to Hamid's cousin. He looked and sounded exactly like Shakil. Or as Shakil would if he'd sloughed off his laid-back, live-for-the-moment attitude and aged a few years.

This man had a thinner face, which accentuated his superb bone structure. And his expression was grim, far harder than anything Shakil had ever worn. Shakil had been a lover not a fighter and this man looked, despite his western tailoring, as if he'd be at home on a warhorse, a scimitar in his hand as he galloped into battle.

Arden shivered, clammy palms skimmed her bare arms as she tried to ease the tension drawing gooseflesh there.

He said something. She saw his lips move, but there was a weird echoing in her head and she couldn't make out his words.

She blinked, swaying forwards, stumbling and steadying herself, drawn unwillingly by his dark velvet gaze.

Hamid pulled her against his side. 'I'm sorry. I shouldn't have insisted you come tonight. Your condition is too delicate.'

Arden stiffened in his hold, dimly noting the Sheikh's sharply indrawn breath. Hamid was a dear friend but he had no right to feel proprietorial. Besides, it was a long time since she'd craved any man's touch.

'I'm perfectly healthy,' she murmured, trying to inject power into the words. The flu had knocked her but she was almost back to normal. Yet her recent illness provided a perfect explanation for her woozy head and unsteady legs.

She moved a half step away so he had to drop his arm. Gathering the shreds of her composure, she met the Sheikh's midnight eyes again, instinctively fighting the awareness thundering through her, and the crazy idea she knew him. That wasn't possible. Shakil had been a student, not a sheikh.

'Thank you for the welcome, Your Highness.

It's a beautiful party.' Yet she'd never wanted to leave anywhere with such urgency.

It felt as if he delved right into her thoughts with that unblinking regard. It took all her control not to shift under his scrutiny.

'Are you sure you're well, Ms Wills? You look unsteady on your feet.'

Her smile grew strained and she felt the tug of it as her face stiffened.

'Thank you for your concern. It's only tiredness after a long week.' Heat flushed her cheeks at the realisation she'd actually come close to collapsing for the first time in her life. 'I'm very sorry but I think it best if I leave. No, really, Hamid, I'm okay by myself.'

But Hamid would have none of that. Nothing would satisfy him but to see her home.

'Idris doesn't mind, do you, Cousin?' He didn't wait for an answer but went on. 'I'll at least see you back to the house then return.'

From the corner of her vision Arden registered the sharp lift of the Sheikh's eyebrows, but she had more to worry about than whether she offended by leaving his party early.

Like how she could kindly but effectively stave off Hamid's sudden romantic interest without straining their friendship.

Like how Sheikh Idris could be so uncannily like the man who'd torn her world apart.

And, most important of all, why it was that even

after four years she felt sick with longing for the man who'd all but destroyed her.

A night without sleep did nothing for Arden's equilibrium. The fact it was Sunday, the one day of the week she could sleep in instead of heading in to work at the florist's shop, should have been a welcome pleasure. Instead she longed for the organised chaos of her workday race to get out the door.

Anything to distract from the worries that had descended last night. And worse, the memories, the longings that had haunted each sleepless hour.

Life had taught her the dangers of sexual desire, and worse, of falling in love. Of believing she was special to someone.

For four years she'd known she'd been a naïve fool. Brutal reality had proven it. Yet that hadn't stopped the restlessness, the yearning that slammed into her like a runaway truck the moment she'd looked up into the eyes of Sheikh Idris of Zahrat.

Even now, in the thin light of morning, part of her was convinced he was Shakil. A Shakil who'd perhaps suffered a head injury and forgotten her, like a hero in an old movie with convenient amnesia. A Shakil who'd spent years searching desperately for her, ignoring all other women in his quest to find her.

Sure. And her fairy godmother was due any minute, complete with magic wand and a pumpkin carriage.

Shakil could have found her if he'd wanted. *She* hadn't lied about her identity.

He'd taken pleasure in seducing a gullible young Englishwoman, starry-eyed and innocent, on her first overseas vacation.

Arden shivered and hunched her shoulders, rubbing her hands up her arms.

She was *not* giving in to fantasy. She'd done with that years ago. As for the Sheikh looking like Shakil—it was wishful thinking. Wasn't it Hamid's almost familiar looks that had drawn her to him that day at the British Museum? That and his kind smile and the earnest, self-effacing way he spoke to her about the elaborately beautiful perfume bottles and jewellery at the special exhibition of Zahrati antiquities.

He'd reminded her of Shakil. A quieter, more reserved Shakil. So was it any wonder his cousin the Sheikh had a similar effect? Maybe crisp dark hair, chiselled features and broad shoulders were common traits among the men of their country.

Right now she'd had enough of Zahrati men to last a lifetime. Even Hamid, who'd suddenly turned from friend and landlord to would-be boyfriend. When had that happened? How had she not seen it coming?

Setting her jaw, Arden grabbed an old pullover and shrugged it on, then cautiously opened the cleaning cupboard, careful not to make too much noise. At least, as the only one awake, she had time to ponder what to do about Hamid and his sudden possessiveness.

Grabbing a cloth and the brass polish, she unlatched the front door and stepped outside, pulling it to behind her. She always thought better when she worked. Rubbing the brass door knocker and letter box would be a start.

But she hadn't begun when she heard footsteps descend to the pavement from the main house door above her basement flat. A man's steps. Arden took the lid off the polish and concentrated on swiping some across the door knocker. She should have waited till she was sure Hamid had left. But she'd felt claustrophobic, cooped up inside with her whirling thoughts.

'Arden.' The voice, low and soft as smoke, wafted around her, encircling like an embrace.

She blinked and stared at the glossy black paint on the door a few inches from her nose. She was imagining it. She'd been thinking of Shakil all night and—

Footsteps sounded on the steps leading down to the tiny courtyard in front of her basement home.

She stiffened, her shoulders inching high. This wasn't imagination. This was real.

Arden swung around and the tin of polish clattered to the flagstones.

CHAPTER TWO

HUGE EYES FIXED on him. Eyes as bright as the precious aquamarines in his royal treasury. Eyes the clear green-blue of the sea off the coast of Zahrat.

How often through the years had he dreamed of those remarkable eyes? Of hair like spun rose gold, falling in silken waves across creamy shoulders.

For a second Idris could only stare. He'd been prepared for this meeting. He'd cancelled breakfast with Ghizlan and their respective ambassadors to come here. Yet the abrupt surge of hunger as he watched Arden Wills mocked the belief he was in command of this situation.

Where was his self-control? How could he lust after a woman who belonged to someone else?

To his own cousin?

Where was his sense, coming here when he should be with the woman to whom he was about to pledge his life?

Idris didn't do impulsive any more. Or self-centred. Not for years. Yet he'd been both, seeking out this woman to confirm for himself what

Hamid had implied last night—that they lived together.

A ripple of anger snaked through him, growing to gut-wrenching revulsion at the idea of her with his cousin.

'What are you doing here?' Her voice was husky, evoking long ago memories of her crying out his name in ecstasy. Of her beguiling, artless passion. Of how she'd made him feel for a short time, like someone other than the carefree, self-absorbed youth he'd been.

How could such ancient memories feel so fresh? So appallingly seductive?

It had only been a holiday romance, short-term fun such as he'd had numerous times. Why did it feel different?

Because it *had* been different. For the first time ever he'd planned to extend a casual affair. He hadn't been ready to leave her.

'Hamid's away.' Was that provocative tilt of her jaw deliberate, or as unconscious as the way her fingers threaded together?

Satisfaction stirred. It was beneath him perhaps, but reassuring to discover he wasn't the only one on edge. Idris was used to being sure of his direction, always in command. Doubt was foreign to him.

'I didn't come here to see Hamid.'

Those eyes grew huge in a face that looked even milkier than before. Hamid had talked of her being *delicate.* Was that code for pregnant? Was that why she looked like a puff of wind would knock her over?

Jealousy, a growling caged beast, circled in his belly. It didn't matter that he had no right to feel it. Idris had stopped, somewhere around four this morning, trying to tell himself he felt nothing for Arden Wills. He was a pragmatist. The fact was he did *feel*. He was here to sort out why and then, with clinical precision, to put an end to it.

'You should sit. You don't look well.'

'I'm perfectly fine.' She crossed her arms, making Idris aware of the swell of plump breasts under her shapeless pullover. Had her breasts always been like that? He remembered them as delectable, but—

'I'm up here.' A palm waved in front of his eyes and, for the first time he could recall, Idris felt embarrassment at being caught ogling. Heat flushed his face. It wasn't a sensation to which he was accustomed.

When he lifted his gaze he saw a matching bright pink stain on her cheeks. Annoyance? Embarrassment? Or something akin to the untimely, unwanted attraction he couldn't quash?

'I came to see you.' His voice dropped to a primal, darkly possessive note he couldn't hide.

'Me?' Now she was on the back foot and, ridiculously, it pleased Idris. He hated the sensation, since last night, that he careered out of control.

'You. Shall we go inside?'

Her folded arms dropped, spreading out a little from her body, almost as if she'd bar his entry to the house. 'No. We can speak here.'

Idris scowled. 'Surely even in Britain one invites guests inside?'

Her mouth tightened but she remained defiant. 'I prefer to stay outside. It's…better.' She took a step back. To prevent him hauling the door open?

Idris felt his head snap back as if he'd been slapped. Did she have so little faith in his chivalry? Was she really afraid to be alone with him?

He was torn between delight at the idea he wasn't the only one feeling the burn of rekindled lust and horror that his feelings were reciprocated and therefore harder to quell.

'I have a key to Hamid's house, if you'd like me to let you in upstairs. Since you're his cousin, I'm sure he wouldn't mind.'

Idris jerked his gaze up to the glossy black door a level above them, and then to the one behind Arden, noting for the first time the brass street number with a small but significant letter A beside it. The relief washing through him was palpable.

'You live in a basement flat? You don't live together?'

She drew herself up till she almost topped his shoulder. Idris told himself the movement wasn't endearing, yet he felt a little corkscrewing twist of pleasure that punctured his satisfaction in an instant.

'We don't live together. Hamid is my landlord.'

Yet that didn't mean they weren't lovers. For all Hamid's devotion to history and old books, he, like every other male in their family, had a penchant for a pretty face and a delectable female body. Besides, there'd been no mistaking Hamid's proprietorial attitude last night, or his meaning when he'd spoken about a *special* woman in his life.

'It's you I came to see.'

She shook her head and a froth of hair swung around her, the colour of the desert at sunrise. Last night he'd been thrown by the smoothly conventional way she'd worn it. This was the woman he recalled, with a riot of loose curls that made his palms itch to feel all that silken softness.

'Why?'

Was she being deliberately obtuse?

'Perhaps to talk over old times?'

There was a thud as she fell back against the solid door, her face a study in shock.

'It *is* you! You were at Santorini.'

Idris stared. 'You thought I was someone else? You didn't remember me?'

It was impossible. He might have had more lovers than he could remember, but the idea Arden Wills had forgotten him was inconceivable.

Especially when his recall of her was disturbingly detailed. After four years he still remembered the little snuffling sigh she made in her sleep as she snuggled, naked, against him. The feel of her slick, untried body when they'd made love the first time returned to him time and again in his dreams. He'd almost exploded disgracefully early at the sheer erotic enticement of her delicate, tight body and the knowledge he was the first man to introduce her to ecstasy. Doing his duty and walking away from her had been amazingly difficult.

'I thought…' She shook her head, frowning. 'How can you be a sheikh? You were a student.'

'Ex-student—I'd just finished a graduate degree in the States when we met. As for becoming Sheikh—' he shrugged '—my uncle died. It was his wish that I succeed him and that wish was ratified soon after his death.'

It sounded easy, but the reality had been anything but. He was a different man to the one he'd been four years ago. Responsibility for a country that had suffered so long because of its ruler's neglect had transformed him. He carried the burden of changing his homeland into one ready to face the future instead of dwelling on the past. This morning was the first time in years he'd carved time to do something simply because he wished it. His secretary's disbelieving look when he'd altered his schedule had spoken volumes.

Idris took a step closer, his nostrils flaring at the astringent smell of metal polish and something more delicate that tickled his memory—the scent of orange blossom.

'Come, let's take this conversation indoors where we can—'

'No!' Her eyes were round as saucers and if it weren't ridiculous he'd say she was shaking.

That brought him up short. He might be supreme ruler of his kingdom and an emerging force in regional politics, but he wasn't the sort of man who deliberately intimidated women.

'I have nothing to say to you, *Your Highness*.' She all but sneered his title and Idris scowled. It hit him suddenly that, for all they'd shared, there was a lot he'd never learned about her.

'You have a problem with royalty?'

She tossed her head back. He couldn't remember her being feisty before, just warm and eager for him. 'I have a problem with men who lie about who they are.'

Idris's hands clenched and his jaw hardened. He wasn't used to having his will crossed, much less his honour impugned. The fact they were having this conversation metres from a public footpath, albeit in a quiet square, incensed him.

His fingers itched with the urge to haul this spitfire of a woman into his arms and barge through the door into her private domain.

Except he knew in the most primitive, instinctive part of his brain that if he touched her he was in danger of unleashing something far better left alone.

He'd come here to satisfy his curiosity and put an end, somehow, to the nagging sense of unfinished business between them.

He was about to become betrothed to a beautiful, diplomatically desirable princess. Their match was eagerly awaited by both nations. Getting involved in any way with Arden Wills would be a mistake of enormous proportions. Giving in to the dark urge to lay hands on her and remind her how it had been between them with a short, satisfying lesson in physical compatibility would be madness.

And so tempting.

'I never lied,' he said through gritted teeth.

Dark gold eyebrows rose in a deliberately offensive show of disbelief that stirred the anger in his belly.

'No? So you're telling me you're not Sheikh Idris? Your name is actually Shakil?'

'Ah.' He'd forgotten that.

'Yes, ah!' She made it an accusation, looking down that little nose of hers as if he were some lowlife instead of a paragon of duty and honour. No one had ever looked at him that way.

'I used Shakil when we met because—'

'Because you didn't want me finding you again.' The words spat out like poisoned darts. 'You had no intention of following through on that promise to meet again, did you? You'd already wiped your hands of me.'

'You accuse me of lying?' No man, or woman, for that matter, had ever doubted his word.

Arden crossed her arms over her chest and tipped her chin up in a supercilious expression as full of hauteur as that of any blue-blooded princess. 'If the shoe fits.'

Idris took a step closer before his brain kicked into gear and screamed a warning. Ire overcame the seductive tug of that orange blossom scent. Caution disappeared on the crisp breeze eddying down from street level.

'Shakil was my family nickname. Ask Hamid.' It meant *handsome* and was one he discouraged, but back then it had been a handy pseudonym. He heaved a deep breath, telling himself he didn't care that the movement reduced the distance between them. Or that his nostrils flared as the scent of warm female flesh mingled with the fragrance of orange blossom. 'I used Shakil on vacation to avoid being recognised. There'd been a lot of media speculation about me and I wanted to be incognito for a while. I was Shakil to everyone I met on that trip. Not just you.'

He'd grown tired of people clamouring for attention because of his royal ties and wealth. Merging into the holiday throng in Greece as Shakil had been a delicious freedom. And it had been a heady delight knowing that when pretty little Arden had smiled at him in that bar on Santorini there'd been stars, not dollar signs in her eyes. She saw simply the man, not the shadow of his family connections and how she might benefit from them.

Was it any wonder he remembered their affair as special?

Still she didn't look convinced.

'As for not turning up at the rendezvous that last afternoon—you can hardly hold me to account. You didn't show.'

A phone call had hauled him out of Arden's bed and back to the upmarket hotel room where he hadn't spent a single night for the week since he'd met her. All he'd known at first was something important had happened and he needed privacy to talk with his uncle's closest advisers. It was only when he was alone in his hotel that he'd learned about his uncle's heart attack, the fact his life hung by a thread, and that he'd named Idris his heir.

There'd been no question of returning to the rendezvous with Arden—three o'clock by the church—even if she had decided to accept his invitation to an extended vacation in Paris. There'd been no question of Paris or a lover, not when he was urgently needed at home.

And if he'd been fleetingly disappointed that she'd thought better of accepting his offer, he'd known it made things easier given the enormity of what he faced. He had enough experience of clinging women to know severing ties could be tiresome.

'You went to the church to meet me?' Her words held a breathless quality and there was something in her eyes he couldn't read.

'I had to fly home urgently. I sent someone instead.'

There was a tiny thud as her head rocked back against the door. Her eyes closed and her mouth twisted. Idris frowned at what looked like pain on her features.

'Are you okay?'

'Fine.' Finally she opened her eyes. 'Absolutely fine.'

She didn't look it. She looked... He couldn't put a name to that expression, yet he felt an echo of it slap him hard in the chest.

'He didn't wait long.'

'Sorry?'

'Your friend. He didn't stay long.'

'You're saying you *did* go to the rendezvous?' To say goodbye or accept his offer of a longer affair? For a moment Idris wondered, until he reminded himself it was history, done and dusted.

'I was late.'

It was on the tip of his tongue to ask why. Second thoughts? A last-minute dash? He pictured her running through the narrow streets of Thera, between the whitewashed buildings she'd so enjoyed exploring. Her hair would be down like now, and her summer skirt floating around those lissom legs.

He chose to say nothing. What was there to say now, after four years? What was done was done.

Except, remarkably, it seemed that what they'd shared in that sultry week in Santorini hadn't quite ended.

Arden Wills wasn't dressed to seduce. Her dark green pullover swam on her, just hinting at the curves beneath. Her old jeans were frayed and there was a patch on one knee. Her face was free of make-up. Yet her hair rippled around her like a halo on a Pre-Raphaelite model, beguiling and exotic. She made him want to forget duty, forget necessity, and tug her to him so she fitted between his thighs, cradling him with her hips.

'So, what is it you want?'

'Pardon?' Idris shoved his hands deep into his trouser pockets as he realised the direction his thoughts wandered. To whether she wore a bra beneath that bulky pullover and whether her pale skin was as petal-soft as he recalled.

'Why did you come here, if not to see your cousin?' She paused, her lips tightening. 'Surely not to catch up on old times.' Her breathing altered, drew short and jerky, as if she, too, remembered how it had been between them all those years ago.

'Why not?' Idris lifted his shoulders in a show of insouciance he was far from feeling. 'I was...

curious about you. It's been, what? Four years?'
As if he didn't know precisely how long it had
been. His reign as Sheikh of Zahrat dated from that
week. 'There have been changes in both our lives.'

Her face stilled, her eyes darting to the side almost furtively, as if tempted to look behind her
but thinking better of it.

Instantly Idris was on alert.

He couldn't read that look but instinct warned
him something was afoot. Something she hid from
him. His gaze lifted to the gleaming paint of the
door behind her. What could she possibly feel the
need to hide? She wasn't living in squalor, not here.
Something sordid? A lover?

Adrenalin surged, coiling his tension tighter. He
took another half step forward, only stopping when
a small palm flattened against his chest. He felt
the imprint of it through the fine wool of his suit.
His skin tingled where she touched as if abraded.
As if she'd scraped sharp nails over his bare flesh.

Idris sucked in oxygen and forced himself not
to react.

'I don't want you here.' Those eyes were so huge
in her face he felt he could dive into them.

His hand covered hers and fire danced across
his skin before burrowing deep inside. A judder of
potent sexual hunger tightened his groin.

'You need to say that as if you mean it.'

The scent of her was so vivid he could almost
taste her on his tongue. Sweet with a telltale hint

of warm musk. No woman before or since had smelled like Arden Wills. How had he forgotten that?

'I do mean it.' Yet her voice had a soft, wondering quality that reminded him of the night they'd shared their bodies that first time. Her eyes had shone with something like awe. She'd looked at him as if he were a glorious deity opening the secrets of the heavens, until her eyes clouded in ecstasy and she'd shattered in a climax so powerful it had hauled him over the edge.

His thumb stroked the back of her hand and she quivered. Her hand was small but strong. He recalled how, as her confidence grew, she'd been as demanding as he, exploring, stroking, driving him to the brink with her generous passion.

She'd driven him to flout his self-imposed rules and invite her to France on holiday with him, because a week together hadn't been enough.

Idris hauled himself back to the present. To the slant of sunlight burnishing her hair and the distant sound of a car. London. His betrothal. The peace treaty between his nation and Ghizlan's.

He shouldn't be here. His life was about duty, control and careful, deliberate decision-making. There was no room for spur-of-the-moment distractions.

In another second he'd step away.

But first he needed her to acknowledge what was between them. Even after all this time. Idris couldn't countenance the idea that he alone burned. Pride demanded proof that she felt this undercurrent of hunger. This electricity simmering and snapping in the air. The charge of heat where they touched.

'You need to leave. Don't make me scream for help.' Her head tipped back against the door, as if to increase the distance between them, yet her touch betrayed her. Her hand had slipped under his jacket lapel, fingers clutching his shirt. Heat poured into him from her touch, spreading to fill his chest.

He forced his hand to his side, conquering the impulse to haul her close.

'I said, leave me alone.' Her breath was warm on his chin and his thoughts whirled as he imagined her sweet breath on other parts of his body. He needed a moment to curb his arousal.

Here, on a London street!

Anger flared. At this woman. At his unruly body that for the first time in memory didn't obey.

'It's obviously escaped your notice, but I'm not touching you. *You're* the one touching *me*.'

His voice, crisp with challenge, nevertheless held that once heard and never forgotten deep note that resonated right to her core.

Arden blinked, dragging her gaze from his mouth and solid, scrupulously shaved jaw to his chest.

Heat scorched her cheeks at the sight of her hand clutching him, as if she couldn't bear to let him go. As if, even now, his desertion couldn't kill the slavish passion she'd felt for him.

Though, if he told the truth, he hadn't deserted her.

It was too much to take in.

Too terrible to think that perhaps he hadn't betrayed her as she'd believed.

Words trembled on her tongue, the truth she hadn't been able to share with this man for four years. But caution held her back.

She needed time alone to sort out what it meant if he *hadn't* deserted her. Time away from his piercing dark gaze and hot body that reduced her hard won defences to ash.

Arden dragged her hand away, pressing it against the solid door behind her. That was what she needed. To remember where they were and how much was at stake. She couldn't risk revealing too much.

'You need to go. This isn't right.' A weight lodged on her chest, making her breathless so she could only manage short sentences.

Something that might have been anger flickered across his face. Yet still he didn't shift.

Desperation coiled tight in her belly. A desperation fuelled by the urge to spill everything to him, here and now, as if by doing so all her burdens would be lifted.

But Arden had spent a lifetime learning self-reliance. The last years had reinforced that. She carried her burdens alone.

'We've both moved on, Shakil.' It was as if she evoked the past with that one single word. 'Idris,' she amended quickly.

'Moved on where? To Hamid?' His voice was a low growl that sent fear feathering her skin. His head lowered and she felt tension come off his big frame in waves. 'You're afraid your lover will see us together?'

'Don't be ridiculous.' It came out as a hiss of distress. It had been bad enough realising last night that Hamid now saw himself as far more than a friend.

'Ridiculous?' Idris's eyes narrowed to ebony slits. Those carved cheekbones loomed threateningly high as his face drew taut. 'You call me ridiculous?'

Fire branded her neck as hard fingers closed around her nape, moulding to skin turned feverish at his touch.

Arden swiped her suddenly arid mouth with her tongue, searching for words to stop the fury in that glittering gaze.

But his touch didn't feel like anger. That was the problem. She could have withstood it if it did.

Arden trembled as the hand at her neck shifted and long fingers speared her hair, spreading over her scalp, massaging. Shivers of delight rippled through her and her eyelids hovered, weighted, at half mast. Tendrils of fire cascaded from her scalp down her spine and around to her breasts where her nipples peaked.

She swallowed convulsively and forced herself to straighten away from the door, even though it meant brushing against him.

'I didn't mean—'

'Of course you did.' His mouth twisted. 'You're right. It *is* ridiculous. Impossible and inconvenient…and inevitable.'

Then, while Arden was still absorbing his words, his head lowered.

His mouth on hers was just as she remembered. A huge, tearing fullness welled in her chest as his lips shaped hers, not hard and punishing as she'd expected from the glint in his eyes, but gentle, questing. As if seeking an answer to a question she hadn't heard.

Shakil. The taste of him burst on her, rich and delicious. It was the one sense memory she hadn't been able to recall in the years since he'd left her. Now it filled her, evocative, masculine and, she feared, potently addictive. For her head was lolling back, lips open to allow him access.

Somehow her hands had crept up to brace on his chest. The steady thrum of his heart was a reassuring counterpoint to her sense of disorientation.

His other hand slipped around her waist, pulling her against a body that was all hard power, making her feel soft and feminine in ways she'd almost forgotten.

And still that kiss. No longer quite as gentle. Arden heard a guttural sound of approval as her tongue met his in a foray into pure pleasure.

He shifted and delight filled her as her nipples grazed his torso. She moved closer, absorbed in heady, oh-so-familiar delight, till a long hard ridge pressed against her belly.

Arden's eyes snapped open and she saw his eyes had narrowed to slits of dark fire. Then, over his shoulder, high up at street level, came a burst of light, a glint of sunlight off something. It was enough, just, to bring her back to reality.

'No.' No one heard her protest since their lips were locked.

She had to shove with all her might for him to lift his head, blinking as if unable to focus. That might have made her feel better but for the realisation that just five minutes in this man's company had obliterated every defence she'd spent years constructing.

'No,' she gasped. That full feeling behind her breastbone turned to pain. 'This is wrong. We can't...'

She didn't need to go on. Sheikh Idris of Zahrat agreed completely. It was there in the dawning horror sharpening his features and the unsteady hand that swiped his face. He shook his head as if wondering what he was doing.

Nor did Arden need to shove him again. One swift pace backwards on those long legs took him almost to the base of the area steps and left her feeling appallingly alone.

Chest pumping, Arden stared at the dark-gold face of the man she'd once adored. The man who now looked at her as if she were his personal nightmare.

Desperate, she put her palms to the door behind her, needing its support.

Despite it all, the anger, hurt and betrayal that had shaped her life for four years, she'd harboured a hope that if they met again he'd admit he'd made a terrible mistake in leaving. That he'd missed her, wanted her, as she'd missed and wanted him.

In her dreams he'd never looked at her with horror.

Pain lanced her chest and kept going right down through her womb.

With a choking gasp of distress she whirled around, hauled the door open and slipped into her sanctuary. Her hands shook so much it took for ever to bolt and latch the door. When it was done Arden put her back to it and slid down to sit on the floor, arms wrapped around her knees as silent sobs filled her.

CHAPTER THREE

'YOUR HIGHNESS, IF I may?'

Idris looked up from the papers on the ambassador's desk. His aide, Ashar, stood in the doorway, expression wooden. That, Idris had learned in the turbulent first few years of his rule, was a sure sign of trouble.

Please, not another delay with the combined peace and trade treaty. Ghizlan's father might be eager to cement a dynastic bond with Idris but he wasn't past trying to wheedle more concessions before the betrothal was announced.

Idris turned to the ambassador, who, ever the diplomat, was already standing. 'If you'll excuse me, Highness, I'll leave you to check for news on that US investment project.'

Idris nodded. 'That would be useful, thank you.'

When the ambassador had left, Ashar entered the room, closing the door behind him. Silently he passed a computer tablet across the desk. Bold black lettering filled the screen.

Off the Leash in London, Sheikh Tastes Local Delicacies.

Beneath the headline was a photo. A close-up of Idris locked in an embrace with Arden Wills, her hair a riot of curls against the black of her front door.

The air rushed from his lungs as an unseen punch slammed a sickening blow into his mid-section.

Damn it. Hadn't he known it was a mistake, going to her house? Hadn't it defied logic? Yet when she'd told him to leave, what had he done? Had he behaved like the sane, prudent man he was and returned to his embassy? No, he'd reacted like...like...

Words failed.

Worse was the fact that, facing a nightmare public debacle, he had total recall of her sweet mouth and her soft body moulding to his.

'There's more.'

Of course there was. It was the way of the world that you slaved twenty hours a day for your country and the first time in four years you did something utterly selfish, utterly incomprehensible, the press was there to turn a molehill into a mountain.

He sighed and forked his hand through his hair. 'Let me guess. Princess Ghizlan.'

He scrolled to the next page and the next headline.

Two-Timing Sheikh Keeps Fiancée and Lover in Same City.

Idris swore long and low. There was a photo of him and Ghizlan at the embassy reception. Beside it was one of him with Arden. His hand wrapped around her neck, pulling her to him, and her eyes were closed, those plump lips open, as if eager for his kiss. As if she hadn't just told him to take a hike.

Fire shot from his belly to his groin. Even now, with all hell about to break loose, his body was in thrall to the Englishwoman he should have forgotten four years ago. Instead he remembered it all. She'd been ardent, so deliciously honest and real. Her desire had been for *him*, not his wealth or connections. Together they'd created a magic he'd craved more of, though brutal logic said it must eventually burn out. Passion always did. That was how it always was for the men in his family, how it was for him—lust and desire, never anything more permanent.

He shoved the tablet across the table and shot to his feet, stalking away from the desk.

Of all the impossible timing. This was the worst. For his country, and for Ghizlan's.

Ghizlan! He'd put her in an appalling situation.

'Get me the Princess on the phone.' He spun around. 'No. Contact her aide and ask for a meeting. I'll come to her hotel immediately.'

Ashar didn't move. 'There's more.'

'More? How could there be more? There *was* nothing else. That—' he gestured to the photo of him hauling Arden into his arms '—is the sum total of what happened.'

His jaw was so rigid it felt as if it might shatter. Self-contempt swamped him.

How often had he told himself he was better than his uncle, the old Sheikh, who'd frittered his time and energy on endless lovers instead of governing? Or Idris's father, whose philandering destroyed his family and any respect he might have garnered from the people?

Idris had taken pride in devoting himself to his people, putting duty before pleasure. His planned marriage to Ghizlan was for the good of both nations. He'd modelled himself on the one completely honourable man in his family, his grandfather. The old man had been the sole exception in six generations to the rule that men in his family couldn't love. Idris didn't expect a miracle—to love one woman all his life like his grandfather had. But he aimed at least to be loyal to his wife. A great start he'd made on that!

'There's something you should see before you talk to the Princess.'

Ashar's expression was as grave as on the day Idris had returned home to find his uncle on his deathbed.

Idris put out his hand for the tablet. 'Show me.'

Ashar scrolled to another page, then passed it to him, half turning away as he did so.

Idris frowned. It felt almost as if Ashar was trying to give him privacy. The notion was laughable. His aide knew as many diplomatic and royal secrets as he did. More probably.

Then Idris looked down and felt the floor buckle beneath his feet.

Royal Baby Secret. Which Cousin Did Arden Seduce?

This time there were three photos. One of his cousin Hamid entering college with a briefcase in his hand. One of Idris in traditional robes, taken at some public event.

And one of Arden Wills holding a toddler in her arms.

Idris felt his eyes bulge as he took in the details. Arden's attention was on the child throwing bread to some ducks. A child whose face was golden, in contrast with her ivory and rose features. A child with glossy black hair and dark eyes.

A child with a remarkable resemblance to Idris at that age.

Or his cousin.

Idris tried to read the words beneath the photos but they blurred into lines of swarming black ants. He blinked and ordered himself to focus, but his eyes were drawn to that telling photo. Arden smiling radiantly at a child who, Idris would bet his sword arm, belonged to the royal family of Zahrat.

Sensation bombarded him and he had to brace his feet so as not to collapse back into the leather chair.

How old was the child? He knew nothing of babies. Two? Three?

Could it be his?

Shock scattered his thoughts. He should be planning an appropriate public response, deliberating on the fallout and talking to his almost-fiancée.

Instead he stared at the photo with something like possessiveness.

He was marrying partly to secure an heir but becoming a father was a political necessity, not a heartfelt desire. His own father had been distant and Idris knew little about good father-child relationships. He'd assumed his wife would take the lead in child-rearing.

Yet, looking into the laughing face of a child that might be his, Idris was gripped by a surge of protectiveness he'd never before experienced. This could be his son or daughter. The idea slammed into him like a physical blow, stealing his breath and obliterating any illusion of disinterest.

'Boy or girl?'

'A boy. She named him Dawud.' Not an English name then. There was obvious significance in that.

'Dawud.' An unseen cord tugged at his heart, making it thud faster.

Why hadn't she contacted Idris? Why keep his existence a secret? Anger stirred amidst the glowing embers of softer emotion.

Unless he's not yours.

Remember Hamid last night, his 'someone special'. Arden was living under his roof.

Yet if Hamid was the father, why not claim the child as his own? Hamid might have inherited the family practice of sowing his wild oats, but he had a serious side. He wouldn't shirk responsibility, especially if he cared for Arden as he seemed to.

Idris stared at the photo, trying to read the truth in the curve of the child's chubby cheek and wide smile.

That was when he realised his hand was shaking. And the feeling snaking through his belly wasn't mere curiosity but something perilously close to jealousy. At the thought of Hamid and Arden.

Idris dropped the tablet onto the desk and scrubbed a hand over his face.

Did he *want* the scandal of an illegitimate child? A child whose first, vital years he'd missed?

He'd have to be crazy.

His phone was in his hand before he realised. He called Hamid's number and looked up, surprised, to see the sun still streaming through the high sash windows. It felt as if time had galloped since Ashar had entered the room.

No answer from Hamid, just the message bank. It took far too long for Idris to remember his cousin mentioning an early flight to an academic conference in Canada. He was probably in the air, absorbed in one of his beloved journal articles.

Idris swung around to Ashar. 'Anything else?'

Ashar's lips twitched in what might in another man have edged towards a smile. 'That's not enough?'

'More than enough.' Scandal in London and no doubt at home, as well as in Ghizlan's country. A betrothal contract about to be signed, a peace treaty on the table and a child who might be his.

And, simmering beneath it all, the taste he hadn't been able to banish from his memory. The sweet taste of Arden Wills, sabotaging his ability to concentrate.

'Get me the Princess's suite on the line. And send a security detail to my cousin's house.'

'To keep the press back? They'll already be there in droves.'

'To observe and report back. I want to know what's going on.'

Whether the child was his cousin's or his own, Idris had a responsibility to protect mother and child from the notoriously intrusive paparazzi. At least till he sorted out the truth.

'And find out what time my cousin's flight touches down in Canada. I want to talk to him as soon as he lands. Get someone to meet the flight.'

* * *

Arden ignored the pounding on the front door, turning up the television so Dawud could hear the music of his favourite children's programme. He sat enthralled, bouncing while he clapped his hands in time with the music.

When the reporters had descended on the house he'd cried, awakened from his nap by the hub-bub of voices and the constant noise of the phone and knocking at the front door. Arden felt wobbly with frustrated outrage because even now they hadn't left.

She'd been more than reasonable. She'd gone to the door and asked politely for some privacy. She'd given a 'no comment' response to their frenzy of questions and faced their clicking cameras, giving them the pictures they wanted.

But it hadn't been enough. They'd clamoured to see Dawud. They'd even known his name. That was when anger had turned ice-cold, freezing her from the inside out.

She wouldn't let those vultures near her precious boy. They'd mobbed her, trying to follow her into her basement flat. Terror had grabbed her as she slammed the door shut, her hands slick with sweat.

She'd turned to find Dawud watching, eyes huge and bottom lip trembling, as the noise echoed through their little home.

There had to be a way out of this. Somewhere to escape. But Hamid was overseas and her friends had no more resources than she did. Certainly not enough to spirit her and Dawud away.

A shudder racked her. She needed to find somewhere safe till this died down. How she was going to do that when she was due at work tomorrow she had no idea. Would the reporters hound her at the shop, or mob Dawud's nursery?

Probably both. Her stomach roiled and nausea stirred.

She'd known she shouldn't have gone to that embassy reception. Not because she'd suspected for a moment she'd see Shakil... Idris as he now was. But because it was pure weakness to give in to her curiosity about his country. Look where it had got her.

It's not your fault, it's his. He was the one who kissed you. He was the one who wouldn't leave.

Yet, if she were truthful, those moments in his arms had been magic, as if—

A sharp knock sounded on the front door. That was when Arden suddenly realised how quiet it had grown. As if the crowd of reporters had left.

She didn't believe it for an instant. It was a trick to lure her out, preferably with Dawud.

Arden smiled at her son as he looked up at her, singing the simple lyrics they often sang together. She hunkered down and cuddled him, joining in.

But the rapping on the door started again. Peremptory. Unavoidable.

Kissing Dawud's head, she got up and walked

softly into the tiny entrance hall, closing the door behind her. The letter box flap opened. She hadn't thought of that. She was just wondering what she could use to stick it closed when she heard a man's voice. A deep, assured voice that had featured in her dreams far too often in the last four years.

'Arden. Open the door. I'm here to help.'

Her feet glued to the floor. She was torn between the offer of help and the knowledge that this was the man who'd brought disaster crashing down on them.

And the fact that, despite a sleepless night, she was no closer to knowing if she wanted him in Dawud's life.

As if you've got a choice now.

In the background she heard a rising murmur of voices, presumably from the paparazzi. Yet he didn't speak again. Perhaps because he was used to minions running to obey his every whim. Yet she understood how much courage it took to stand there alone, with a mob of press recording his every move.

And he'd come to help.

She reached out and unlatched the door, staying behind it as she swung it open just wide enough for him to enter.

Swiftly he bolted the door then turned.

Idris. He was definitely Sheikh Idris now. There was no hint of Shakil, the laughing, passionate lover she'd known in Santorini. This man's face was a symphony in sombre beauty, lines carving the corners of his mouth, ebony eyebrows straight and serious.

'You're all right? Both of you?'

Arden nodded. To her dismay her mouth crumpled. Until now she'd been buoyed by fury and indignation. But one hint of concern and she felt a great shudder pass through her. She hadn't realised before how her anger had masked terror.

'Arden.' He reached out as if to take her arm then stopped. His mouth flattened and he dropped his hand.

'We're okay.' Her voice was husky. She told herself she'd react this way to sympathy from anyone after facing the press onslaught. It had nothing to do with the concern in his dark eyes. Yet that look ignited a new warmth in her frozen body.

Finally her brain engaged and she frowned.

'You shouldn't have come. You've made it a hundred times worse. What were you thinking?'

His eyebrows rose in astonishment. Clearly he wasn't used to anyone questioning his actions.

'It can't get any worse. Not after the photos they've already got.' He folded his arms over his dark suit, for all the world like a corporate raider contemplating a run on his stocks, not a Middle Eastern potentate. Surely sheikhs wore long robes and headscarves?

'But now they've seen you here they'll think—'

'They already *know*.' His tone was so grim it

made the tiny hairs at her nape stand up. 'In fact—' he paused, his voice dropping to a silky, dangerous note that made her think of an unexploded bomb '—some would say they know more than I do.'

Arden wanted to say the press didn't know anything. They assumed. But it was splitting hairs.

'Couldn't you have sent someone instead?' She crossed her arms tight across her chest, where her heart catapulted like a mad thing against her ribs. Grateful as she was for assistance, she refused to feel guilty about what had happened. This wasn't down to her. *He* was the one who'd attracted press attention. She was a nonentity.

'I did send someone. But they reported you were surrounded. Your phone is switched off and I assumed that if a stranger knocked on your door, claiming to represent me, you'd think it was a ruse to get you out to face the cameras.' Ebony eyes held hers, challenging.

Reluctantly Arden nodded. He was right. She'd never have opened the door to anyone she didn't know.

'I had to come. There was no other choice.'

How did he sound so calm when they were in this mess? Arden couldn't begin to imagine how she and Dawud could go back to their normal, anonymous lives. She wanted to rant, to point the finger of blame at him, but what would that achieve? She had to protect Dawud. There was no time for the luxury of hysteria.

Besides, despite her fine words, she hadn't been forced into that telltale kiss.

Shame filled her. She'd clung to his broad-shouldered frame, losing herself in his sensuality, in the pull of an attraction that was as powerful as it had always been.

Despite the way he'd abandoned her years ago.

Despite the fact he had a fiancée.

Arden hated herself for that. She should be immune to him now. Her stomach dropped and she stepped away, her back colliding with the wall. Determination filled her. She would *not* fall under his spell again.

'What?' His voice was sharp.

'Your fiancée.' The word rasped out, rough-edged.

'Not my fiancée.'

'But Hamid said—'

'Hamid doesn't know everything.' That twist of his mobile mouth looked cruel. As if the words he held back would flay someone alive.

Slivers of ice pricked her all over.

In that instant he morphed from saviour to threat.

She'd been almost relieved to see him but suddenly, as if scales fell from her eyes, she saw him not as the man she'd once loved, or as Hamid's cousin and a potential safe harbour in this press storm, but as an absolute monarch, accustomed to getting whatever he wanted.

Arden licked her lips. 'What do you want?'

Her gaze flicked to the closed sitting room door before she could stop herself. He noticed. Of course he noticed. How could he not hear the muffled children's ditty and guess who was in there?

The fact he hadn't even turned his head towards the other room only scared her more.

Thinking he'd washed his hands of her once their affair was over, even covering his tracks with a false name, she'd believed herself a sole parent in every sense. But Idris was here now, and she realised in dawning horror that she had no idea how he felt about a child. A male child. A child he might consider his heir. A child he might try to take.

Terror dug razored claws into her belly and her stomach cramped so hard she doubled up, gasping. Surely he didn't plan to steal her baby!

'Arden? What is it?' This time he did reach out, long fingers branding her upper arm and sending flames licking through her.

'Don't *touch* me!' It was a hoarse whisper, the best she could do. But it was enough. He reared back as if scalded.

She straightened, forcing herself to stand tall, jutting her chin to lessen the distance between them.

'Tell me what you want.'

Had she just made the biggest mistake of her life, letting Dawud's father into her home? A father who had the power, physically and financially, to take her baby away?

'Tell me!' Heat glazed her eyes. If he thought he was taking Dawud from her, he understood nothing about a mother's love.

Something she couldn't decipher glowed in those narrowed eyes. 'I want to get you and your son to safety, where you won't be bothered by the press. Then, we need to talk.'

Her stomach did that roller coaster dip again. *Talk* didn't sound at all appealing.

But she was out of choices. She and Dawud couldn't stay holed up, hoping the press would leave. They had to go out some time. Idris was her only lifeline. No one else could get them away from the press. She *had* to trust him, for now at least.

'Pack what the pair of you will need for a couple of days. There's a car outside to take you away and one of my men will be posted nearby to make sure none of the paparazzi break in here to get more fodder for a story.'

Arden's jaw dropped. She hadn't thought of that. Of some stranger pawing through their belongings, sullying their home.

'Don't worry. It won't happen. I won't let it.'

Arden snapped her mouth closed, reeling at his absolute conviction. Never in her life had she been able to rely on anyone. Every time she'd begun to trust she'd been let down. Her parents, foster parents, even Hamid, pretending there was more to their friendship than existed.

There was something inherently appealing about Idris's assurance. Just as well she knew better than to depend on him. But, for the moment, she and Dawud needed help.

'Give me ten minutes.' She started down the hall then stopped, hesitating outside the sitting room door.

'Don't worry. I'll wait here.' It was as if he read her mind, her worry about Dawud.

She hesitated, unable to dismiss the thought of him simply striding in, picking up Dawud and carrying him out of the door.

'You are both safe with me.' That deep voice mesmerised—so grave, so measured. She badly wanted to trust him. He took a single step nearer. 'You have my word, Arden.'

She caught the velvet brown of his eyes that from a distance looked pure black. She read determination in his jaw, strength in his proud stance and honesty in his direct gaze. For a second longer she wavered. Then she spun on her heel and darted into the bedroom.

She'd hear if he tried to scoop up Dawud and take him. Dawud would yell and it would be impossible to exit quickly with that mob outside.

Yet relief hit when she emerged to find him still in the hall. He stood, head bent as if listening to Dawud's high voice carolling enthusiastically.

Arden dropped the two bags, a bulky one full of Dawud's toys and clothes and a small one for her.

Idris's head jerked up. 'Ready?'

Arden nodded, trying and failing to read his expression. 'I'll need a child's car seat and—'

'No need. Arrangements have been made for a car seat. All you need is your bags and your son.'

Your son. Not Dawud. As if Idris was trying to distance himself. Pain turned like a twisting stiletto in her chest. Arden told herself she was pathetic. Seconds ago she'd worried Idris might try to kidnap Dawud. Now she was disappointed he wasn't more enthusiastic about him.

He hasn't even asked if he's the father.

Because this whole situation was a mighty inconvenience for him. More than an inconvenience. Coming just before his marriage to Princess Ghizlan it must be a headache of massive proportions.

She made herself nod and put down the bags. 'I'll get him.'

'You can introduce me.' When she hesitated Idris continued. 'It will make things easier. It will be scary enough for him facing the crowd outside, even with my security men keeping them back.'

Arden hadn't thought of that. It was odd, and unsettling, having someone else point out what her son needed before she did. She couldn't get her brain past the immediate. Right now that was overwhelming. Introducing Dawud to his father. The man she'd thought he'd never know.

The doorknob felt slippery in her clammy hand and she breathed deep, securing a smile for her son. This had to be done and it was up to her to ensure he felt none of the tension crawling up her spine and along her hunching shoulders. Deliberately she pushed back her shoulder blades and walked into the room.

'Mama!' He swung round as the song ended, a huge smile on his face.

Reaction hit her square in the chest as she met his laughing gaze. Eyes of dark brown velvet, so like his father's. When he'd been born they'd been a constant, difficult reminder of the man who'd duped and deserted her. But over the years they'd become simply Dawud's eyes.

Now, seeing the similarities, not just in his eyes but in his whole face, from his jet dark hair to his determined chin, a powerful tide of emotion rose. Arden wobbled to a halt.

'Mama?' Dawud scrambled to his feet and came towards her, arms outstretched. But before he reached her he halted, head turning, eyes growing.

Arden sensed rather than saw Idris beside her. It was as if he generated his own force field, one that made her flesh prickle and tighten whenever he got close.

Was he as nervous as she? As if this were an irrevocable step beyond which the future could never be the same?

She fell to her knees and held her arms out for

Dawud. 'Hello, darling.' Dawud's eyes remained fixed on the man looming over the pair of them, his head craning high to take him in.

Arden was just about to scoop him up when she felt a brush of air beside her as, in a single movement, Idris sank to the floor, settling cross-legged. His knee touched hers but he didn't seem to notice. His attention was fixed on Dawud.

Idris leaned forward a fraction and said something in his own language. Something melodic yet strangely husky, and made a fluid, graceful movement with one powerful hand from his face to his chest.

For a second Dawud stood motionless, then a smile creased his features. 'That!' He pointed at Idris, first his head then his chest.

Idris made the gesture again, slower this time, a courtly gesture of greeting, she realised. Dawud clapped his hands and chuckled, then waved one hand in front of his face, trying to emulate the gesture.

Again that unseen cord tugged at her insides. To watch Dawud smiling at his father, trying to copy him...it was something she'd never expected to see. Not after the hell she'd gone through trying to locate Shakil and finally acknowledging defeat. She didn't even know if she *wanted* to see them together, yet the shining joy in her son's face was hard to resist.

Unwillingly, as if forced by an unseen hand, she

turned her head for a better view. The forbidding majesty who wore hand-made clothes worth more than she earned in six months smiled at Dawud the way Shakil used to smile at her.

Her heart knocked her ribs and dislodged the last of the air in her lungs.

She was still reeling when he turned. Was it imagination or did his eyes glow brighter?

'It's time we left. I can carry Dawud if you like. But my men will keep the paparazzi back so they can't jostle you and Dawud might be happier in your arms than mine.'

Arden nodded. Again he was thinking ahead to the logistics of getting them out of here. Of keeping them safe. She suspected this big man would protect Dawud from all comers. More, he was thinking of Dawud's feelings and his reaction to the stress of change.

A squiggle of heat channelled through her belly and she looked away before he could see how his consideration affected her.

She leaned forward and scooped Dawud into her arms, relishing his scent and the way he snuggled into her. 'Come on, Dimples. We're going out.'

'Man come too.' His gaze was still fixed on Idris.

'Yes, darling. The man will come too.'

The man in question was already on his feet, holding his hand out to help her up. More proof of his thoughtfulness.

But Arden pretended not to notice, scrambling to her feet without assistance.

Touching him was just too unsettling.

Already she feared she was about to walk out of the frying pan and straight into the fire.

CHAPTER FOUR

'WHAT IS THIS PLACE?' Arden had spent most of the
trip focused on Dawud, in the car seat between
her and Idris. Now she looked around the under-
ground garage with its security door to the street
already closing.

'My embassy. You'll be safe here. We approached from the back entrance and weren't followed. My staff ran interference along the route so
the press can't be sure exactly where we've gone.'
He turned and unclipped Dawud's safety harness
as easily as if he'd been doing it for years.

Perhaps he had. The Internet search she'd done
on him after the reception didn't mention a wife
or children but—

Her thoughts frayed as Dawud leaned forward,
reaching for Idris instead of her.

He was a friendly, confident child, but at the
moment, selfishly, she felt a pang at his fascination
with the big man looking down at him so intently.

Then it struck her that though his attention was
fixed on Dawud, Idris hadn't reached out to take

him. Because he felt her qualms? Or because he didn't want to?

Arden lifted her son into her arms, reassured by his warm weight and clean little boy scent.

'I'd prefer a hotel.' She was indebted enough to Idris. More, she knew a foreign embassy was like foreign soil. While here she was in his territory, under his control. Her nerves prickled with foreboding. A spectre of doubt rose. Had she walked into a trap?

Dark eyebrows rose speculatively. 'You'd prefer to run the gauntlet of the press? To hope no hotel employee sells photos of you both to the media?'

Arden gathered Dawud closer, instinctively drawing into the corner of the wide back seat.

'I hadn't thought.' Shock hammered anew and to her horror she began to tremble. It had been a terrible day that got worse by the moment. The picture he painted was as disturbing as the pack of jackals who'd howled questions at them when they got into the car, then tried to follow them down the street.

'It's all right, Arden. There's private accommodation here. You won't be disturbed while we sort out a solution. I can guarantee the discretion of every member of staff.'

Because he was an absolute monarch and he'd have their heads if they betrayed him?

The proud jut of his jaw and the fierce light in his eyes spoke of certainty.

Looking up into a face as hard and beautiful as that of some carved ancient god, Arden felt the terrible imbalance of power between them. He had only to snap his fingers and his staff would obey.

Had she felt this vulnerable facing the paparazzi?

'I need your word first. I want a promise that when I want to leave, with my son, you won't stop us. That we're both free to go.'

For a heartbeat fire pulsed between them. Then his gaze dropped to Dawud. Reflexively her hands tightened and Dawud wriggled, protesting, till she eased her grip. She didn't take her eyes off Idris. Nothing in the world was more important than her son. She'd never let him go.

'You have my word. You're not a prisoner but a guest.' He lifted his gaze to mesh with hers and heat consumed her.

'Come. Let's get the boy settled somewhere more comfortable so we can talk.'

Still Arden hesitated. She was wary of entering his territory. But it was worse than that. Her fear was sparked as much by the way the scent of sandalwood and hot male flesh filled her nostrils, stirring a longing she'd believed herself immunised against. Her body betrayed her with its yearning for a man who'd never be right for her. Even if he'd cared for her, which he hadn't, he was a royal sheikh, a monarch, and she was a single mum from a less than impressive family tree. She didn't belong here.

Frantic thoughts raced. Of her escaping with Dawud in her arms. But to where? Idris and the press would find them.

Idris didn't speak, just sat, watching her as Dawud shifted impatiently and demanded to be put down.

They both knew she was out of options.

Finally, heart heavy, Arden turned towards the door.

Arden had thought the embassy magnificent the night of the reception, with its soaring double storey ceilings topped by intricately glazed domes, its radiant chandeliers and of course the dais with the gilded throne. But she'd assumed the rest of the building would be a little more ordinary.

She'd assumed wrong.

For a start it was even bigger than she'd expected, not one building but several, with a private garden at their centre. Somewhere, she guessed, were offices where staff went about diplomatic duties, but she found herself in a town house, several storeys high and furnished in the luxury she'd seen only in lifestyle magazines.

Yet it wasn't the expensive fittings or exclusive address that impressed; it was the blessed quiet. Peace after the ruckus she'd left behind on her street. Arden hadn't realised how high her anxiety had been till her heartbeat finally eased into something like a normal rhythm.

She settled Dawud into a bright bedroom, spreading out his favourite toys where he could see them. To her surprise Idris didn't insist on that talk to 'sort out a solution'. Instead he left them to relax and explore. Then a young woman with a gentle smile brought a meal for Dawud, explaining the ambassador employed her to care for his children and that she'd been asked to assist, if that was acceptable.

Again Arden was given no cause for complaint. Her consent was sought, though Idris or some super-efficient underling had thought of and provided everything before she even asked.

It was ungrateful to feel *managed*. It was just that she was used to making her own decisions. She was dependent on no one, a lesson learned in childhood. Arden told herself she should learn to accept assistance gratefully, for Dawud's sake. But it was tough.

They had been treated with courtesy and respect. Yet she remembered the fire in Idris's eyes when he spoke of the press knowing more than he about Dawud, and again when he spoke of his cousin, as if there was a rift between the pair. None of that anger had been directed at her.

So far.

No matter how plush the surroundings, she couldn't forget they were in Idris's domain. Were they prisoners despite his promise? Arden shivered, vowing to leave as soon as possible.

Misha, the nanny, offered to sit with Dawud while Arden met 'His Majesty'. Arden was trying to find a reason to put off that meeting when Dawud's drooping eyelids opened wide.

'Man! Hello, man!' He sat up in bed, dimpling as he grinned, and Arden felt a familiar trickle of awareness course from her nape all the way down her spine.

Her breath snagged and her nostrils widened. She told herself she couldn't possibly detect the tang of sandalwood on the air, but her nerves rioted anyway. She swallowed, trying to banish the memory of how Idris had tasted, hot and delicious on her tongue. Not an ancient memory this time but one that was raw and new and all too disturbing.

Reluctantly she turned. Idris leaned in the doorway, immaculate in a dark suit that emphasised his height and hinted at hard-packed strength beneath. His stance was relaxed but there was nothing casual about his expression.

Arden's chest squeezed. He hadn't even noticed her. His attention was fixed on Dawud as if utterly absorbed. The stark intensity of that scrutiny made her stomach churn, as if the squirrels in their local park had invaded her body, leaping and circling faster and faster till she felt nauseous.

He turned, spearing her with that dark gaze,

catching her unprepared. Fire licked inside and she pressed her palm to her belly, only to let it fall, knowing she gave away too much when he followed the movement.

'Everything is satisfactory?'

His calm riled her. She'd been through hell today, and was still scared of what the future held for her son. Yet Idris took it in his stride.

'If you call being hounded by the press satisfactory.' Her lip curled. 'Being forced to hole up here instead of…'

Silence descended as Arden ran out of energy, the air rushing from tight lungs. 'I'm sorry. That's ungrateful.' Even if it *was* his fault, manhandling her like that, especially in public. 'The room is lovely. And Misha—' she turned to smile at the young woman putting away some toys '—has been such a help.'

'Good. Then you have no qualms about leaving Dawud here while we share a meal?'

Of course she had qualms! Arden wanted to go back to the way things had been, just her and her precious boy, safe and secure.

Except then he'd never have a chance to know his father. Despite feeling she teetered on the edge of a very high, very dangerous cliff, Arden knew how important it was for Dawud to grow up supported by both parents. Even the fiasco with the press was worth it if they found a way for him to have a constructive connection with his father.

Apart from anything else, it would be far safer—if anything happened to her, Dawud wouldn't be adrift in the world as she had been.

She recalled the night she'd given birth in a bare hospital room, terrified and alone but for a midwife. She had friends but none close enough to share the intimacy of birth. It had struck her how utterly dependent her baby was on her. She'd vowed to do everything she could to give him love and the sense of belonging she'd been denied as a kid.

'Arden?' Idris took a step closer, frowning.

She blinked. 'Thank you. Dinner would be good.'

'Man!' called an imperious voice. 'I want man.'

'Please,' Arden said automatically.

'Peeze.'

Was that a twitch of Idris's precisely sculpted lips? Before she had a chance to decide, he crossed the room and sat on the edge of Dawud's bed.

Seeing them together, dark heads inclined towards each other, surveying each other with grave interest, Arden's heart gave a silly little flutter. Once, years ago, she'd longed for this, had spent so many hours fruitlessly searching for the man who'd left her pregnant and alone, refusing to believe he'd callously misled her. Until there'd been no alternative.

A hiccupping sigh rose as her little boy brought his hand up to his forehead then swiped it down to his chest, all the while watching the big man before him.

When Idris repeated the gracious gesture of greeting he'd used earlier, Dawud beamed. He swiped his little hand back down from his head in mimicry, this time all the way to his tummy. 'More.'

'Please.' That deep voice was gentle and Arden blinked, feeling foolishly emotional. It had been a long, difficult day. That was all.

'Peeze.'

Idris's mouth hitched up at the corner in a smile Arden had never seen before. A smile that melted a layer of the brittle protection she'd placed around her heart. He repeated the gesture yet again, this time accompanying it with a lilting flow of words in his own language.

His words wove like an exotic, alluring current around the room, mesmerising her, and she wasn't surprised when Dawud leaned closer, obviously rapt.

How long Arden would have sat there, enthralled, she didn't know. But Misha got up, excusing herself to go and tidy up the bathroom after Dawud's enthusiastic splashes.

Suddenly, with her departure, the atmosphere changed. Idris didn't turn but his words this time were clipped.

'I spoke to Hamid. He says the child isn't his.'

Arden blinked and found herself sinking into a nearby armchair.

'Of course he's not Hamid's!' What a crazy idea.

'Is he mine?' Idris asked before she could continue. Again, he didn't face her, but kept his gaze on Dawud. Trying to read her son's parentage in his face?

The sight of Idris's broad back felt like an insult.

'Let me get this straight. You think I went from your bed to your cousin's? What sort of woman do you think I am?'

This time Idris did turn. Unreadable sable eyes pinioned her to her seat. 'I don't know. That's why I ask.'

Arden sagged against the upholstery. Well, that summed up their situation. At twenty she'd spent a week with a man called Shakil and believed she'd met her soulmate, her one true love, and that she knew everything she needed to trust him utterly.

That week had changed her life. Would have changed it even if it hadn't left her pregnant with her precious son. For the first time in years she'd dared to hope, dared to put her trust in someone.

But that life-altering week had clearly been something far...*less* for him. All those passionate words, the promise in his eyes and his touch, his desire to have her with him after Santorini... they'd meant nothing. Nothing except they were physically attracted.

Arden kept her head up as she met his gaze. 'Dawud is your son.'

She waited for some reaction but saw none. Did he feel so little? She'd have sworn she'd read at least a hint of deep emotion when he looked at their little boy. But maybe it was wishful thinking because she so wanted Dawud to be loved by both his parents.

And if he wasn't? She'd give her son so much love and support he'd never notice the lack from his father. Except she, of all people, knew it didn't work like that. Nothing made up for the absence of parents.

Her lip curled. 'I suppose you want a DNA test?'

'It would be sensible, since we're talking about the heir to a kingdom.'

Arden's fingers dug into the padded arms of her chair, biting hard. She told herself he was right. Of course he'd need unassailable proof Dawud was his. Yet it all boiled down to the fact he didn't trust her word.

It took a moment for the rest of his words to hit her. *The heir to a kingdom.* Did Idris intend to acknowledge his son publicly?

Arden was torn between relief that Dawud would have access to both his father and mother and burgeoning fear at what that acknowledgement might mean for their cosy life. Did Idris envisage sharing their son, half the time in the UK and half in Zahrat? The idea of being separated from her baby plunged a dagger through her heart. Until she told herself she was getting ahead of herself.

She looked across to see Idris again talking to Dawud in his own language, even teaching him to say something. Dawud's smile grew and grew as he parroted the simple sounds. Despite her fears, Arden knew that, however difficult this would be for her and Idris, for Dawud, having a family was immeasurably precious.

Misha returned and Idris stood.

'Nigh'-nigh', man.' Dawud opened and closed his hand in his three-year-old's version of a wave.

In response Idris said something first in Arabic, then followed it with, 'Goodnight.'

Arden crossed to the bed and kissed her boy, pushing back his silky dark hair. 'Night-night, sweetie.'

'Nigh'-nigh', Mama.' He pressed his hand to his mouth then flung out his arm in an exuberant kiss that made her smile despite the tension dragging at her belly.

She made herself turn away, reminded Misha to call her if Dawud had trouble settling and followed Idris from the room.

'What was that word you taught Dawud?' Arden asked him across the table laid for two in an intimate dining room.

She looked tired and tense but that didn't

staunch the need dragging low through his body. She hadn't dressed up for dinner with him, wearing jeans and a T-shirt, not even any jewellery. Her only trace of make-up was a clear lipgloss and something to darken her lashes. Yet Idris struggled against the need to touch her.

'*Baba?*' Idris passed her a platter of slow-roasted lamb before taking some.

'That's it. What does it mean?'

She wasn't looking at him as she helped herself to a salad. She hadn't looked at him directly since she'd left the bedroom. As if the sight of him offended.

Was she blind to the fire of attraction crackling between them? Or pretending? Were her plain clothes an attempt to show she wasn't trying to impress? Or that she disdained him?

He didn't know what angered him more, her pretence or that she'd had his child in secret.

The soft lighting turned her hair to spun gold and the tantalising scent of orange blossom drifted to his nostrils. Idris felt his lower body jerk hard.

The fact Arden Wills got under his skin so easily made her dangerous. Idris had no intention of ceding power of any sort to anyone. Not after he'd spent years working day and night to cement his position as the youngest Sheikh in two hundred years. Too much effort had gone into stabilising his nation and building its future.

'*Baba* means Daddy.'

As expected, that got her attention. Her head shot up and once more he felt that jolt as their eyes met. Their kiss had been explosive. It made him wonder what a more intimate touch would be like.

'You don't even know he's yours. Not till you get your paternity test done.' Was that indignation? Certainly there was fire sparking in those extraordinary aquamarine eyes.

The jangling tension inside spread, his blood pumping faster.

Idris shrugged, adopting insouciance to hide his reaction. He wasn't ready to admit he didn't need a scientific test to know Dawud was his son. He couldn't explain his certainty because it defied logic. It wasn't wish fulfilment because, while he'd expected children with Ghizlan, he'd seen that simply as his duty.

Yet he'd looked at the boy and felt something he couldn't explain and had never expected. Certainty was part of it. Happiness, a bright burst of pleasure and protectiveness was another. And relief. Because the idea he'd harboured since seeing the press reports, of Arden and Hamid as lovers, had made him feel wild, out of control.

Idris didn't do out of control. He did planned, logical, well-executed.

'You had no right.'

'Pardon?' He'd lost the thread of her conversation.

'You had no right to tell him you were his father.' Her small, lush mouth was set in a pout that would have been inviting, if not for her abrasive words.

He didn't bother to remind her he'd been speaking his own language, not English, and that the child hadn't understood. But he would soon. Idris would make sure of it.

'*No right?*' He planted his palms on the table and saw her lean back, away from him. 'I have every right. He's, what, three years old? All that time you kept him from me.'

That knowledge had battered him since the moment he'd walked into that basement sitting room and seen his son, a complete stranger yet still his son, sitting on the floor, clapping his hands. It was as if someone had scraped his heart bare, leaving it open and unprotected.

Even when some inner voice had taunted him with the idea the boy could be Hamid's.

'Not by choice. You lied to me about who you were.'

Idris shook his head. 'I told you—I didn't lie. I used an old nickname while I travelled to avoid publicity. I'd been under the microscope because of my family connections and wanted a break, to relax and be like everyone else. I had every intention of explaining who I was if you came with me to Paris.'

It still amazed him that he'd made that offer. But he hadn't been able to get enough of her. Arden's unstinting warmth and zest for life, the way she'd looked at him as if he made the sun shine and the moon rise, had been irresistible.

She didn't look at him that way now.

His jaw set. 'Everything else I told you was true.' Though he'd steered clear of his connection to royalty. 'There was no cause to deny me my son.' He stiffened as he fought the bubbling anger he'd repressed all day.

He flexed his fingers, resisting the urge to reach for her. To shake her into an apology? To kiss her till she stopped hissing at him as if *he* were at fault, not her?

'I didn't keep him from you!' Arden threw her napkin on the table and shoved her seat back.

Idris was on his feet before she was, ready to block the door, determined to have this out. He'd contained himself earlier, knowing the needs of the child had to come first. Patience was a hard won quality. One he'd mastered after assuming the throne, for implementing reform in Zahrat was a slow business. But his patience wore thin. This woman pressed all his buttons.

'Then why not tell me? What did I do on Santorini that convinced you it was better to raise our son alone? How can you justify keeping him from me?' Idris heard the harsh resonance in his voice and hauled in a deep breath. He hated revealing his feelings.

Arden planted her hands on her hips in a provocative stance. Her round chin angled up, her eyes sparked and through her white T-shirt he saw her nipples stand out as hard little points.

He flexed his hands again, resisting the need to reach out and touch. Abruptly he shoved his hands in his pockets.

'How was I supposed to contact you? Tell me that? You hid your tracks too well.'

'I did not—'

'No?' She stalked forward, her face tilted up to meet his. 'I never knew your family name.' She ticked off a finger. 'The one name you gave me was false.' Another finger ticked. 'When I found I was pregnant and contacted the hotel you said you'd booked on Santorini, they refused to confirm you'd been there, much less give me contact details.'

Idris scowled into her angry face. Those security arrangements were normal procedure to protect the privacy of the royal family. It had never occurred that they might have kept Arden from contacting him.

'I had no idea,' he said slowly.

'Sure you didn't.' Her lip curled and she rubbed her arms as if chilled.

About to bite out that hiding from women wasn't his way, Idris paused. If she *had* tried to contact him, how desperate must she have been when she couldn't locate him?

'When you didn't show at the rendezvous I assumed you were happy to walk away.' At the time, he'd had other things on his mind, like suddenly assuming the throne and responsibility for a nation.

'I told you, I did go. Just a little late. At the last minute I couldn't find my passport' Her chin hiked up and those aquamarine eyes held his. 'When the hotel refused to help me contact you I called the Zahrati embassy here in London.' Her mouth twisted and Idris felt a dart of discomfort.

'Do you have any idea how horrible it was, trying to locate you through official channels? All I could tell them was that your name was Shakil, you were twenty-six and spoke excellent English, that you'd studied in the US and you'd once broken your collarbone. I didn't even have photos of you since you were so camera shy.' Her mouth pursed, her nostrils thinning. 'Oh, they were very polite, very kind. I think they felt sorry for me because they guessed why I needed to find you so urgently.'

Heat washed her pale features but her gaze didn't waver. Idris read hurt and defiance there and, if he wasn't mistaken, remembered embarrassment.

What had it been like to discover at twenty that she was pregnant to a stranger? To a man whose real name she didn't even know?

Guilt smote him. It reminded him of the blow he'd received at fourteen, learning traditional battle skills, when he'd been knocked, winded, from his horse and cracked a couple of bones.

Except that had been a clean blow in fair combat. This felt different, tainted with shame, though he hadn't intentionally misled her.

'I'm sorry.' He paused, knowing it wasn't enough. 'I apologise, Arden. What you went through—it must have been devastating. I really do regret that you felt deserted.' Idris stilled. She'd been so young. So bright and innocent. His lungs squeezed hard at the thought of her, scared and alone.

'I never meant to dupe you or hurt you. I only wanted a chance to enjoy myself without attracting public attention.' How selfish and irresponsible that sounded now. 'As for pregnancy, I assumed the precautions we took would be enough.' He felt his shoulders rise. 'I was thoughtless, not even considering repercussions, and for that I apologise again. But believe me, I wasn't trying to hide. Within a week of leaving Santorini I became Sheikh of Zahrat. It never occurred to me you couldn't find me if you needed to.'

Arden stared, her gaze raking as if sifting fact from the lies she'd imagined. 'I had other things on my mind than current affairs. Even if I'd read about it I wouldn't have made the connection between the Shakil I knew and a royal sheikh.'

Idris nodded. How could she have known? How

could either of them? It was no one's fault, just an unfortunate series of circumstances.

Yet that edgy feeling of guilt still lined his gut. He remembered her telling him she had no family. Her parents had died years ago.

'You were okay? Through the pregnancy and birth?' It didn't matter what logic said. Honour dictated he should have been there to provide for her.

Her eyes rounded. 'As you can see, I'm fine.'

Which didn't answer his question. Instead it made him wonder what she hid. Had there been anyone by her side through that ordeal?

'You were well looked after?'

Her gaze hardened. 'I looked after myself. At least I had a steady job to go back to. That supported us both.'

Idris felt her stare like a slap, knowing it was what she didn't say that damned him. He knew next to nothing about childbirth but even he understood women needed support and rest, not just during delivery but after. How soon had she been forced back to work?

'I don't shirk my responsibilities,' Idris said slowly, watching the flash of fire in her eyes. 'If I'd known I would have helped, as I intend to help you now.'

The girl he'd known had been sweet, affectionate and easy-going whereas the woman before him was complicated, feisty and obstinate. Yet her passion and her determination to keep him at a distance only made his hunger for her more acute.

It was inexplicable.

'Good. I always wanted Dawud to know his father. It's important for a child to have a positive relationship with both parents.' She crossed her arms and surveyed him as if considering whether he measured up to her high standards.

Idris paced forward, closing the gap between them.. 'I agree. Which is why we'll marry as soon as possible.'

CHAPTER FIVE

ARDEN STARED UP into dark velvet eyes that glowed in a way she didn't like at all.

It made her think of how he'd hemmed her in against her front door and wrapped his big hand around the base of her skull, holding her captive as he kissed her senseless. And how she'd let him.

Of the heat that shimmered through her every time their eyes met, as if the smallest spark would ignite a conflagration she couldn't douse.

Of the way she'd melted at his touch, his kiss, even his voice.

She didn't want to melt. She wanted to cling to fury at his desertion, believing he'd deliberately dumped her. But, despite her anger and fear, Arden found herself believing the regret in his eyes, the honesty in his voice, the steadfastness in his body language. He hadn't intentionally left her high and dry. He'd sent someone to meet her and she hadn't been there.

An ache opened up in the pit of her belly. The fact it was random circumstance not deliberate intent that had kept them apart somehow seemed almost worse. And now this!

'Marry?' Her voice stretched and splintered.

'Of course. It's the logical solution.'

'Solution? I'm not a problem to be solved!' Easier to let anger hide her curious disappointment.

After all this time did she still pine for the fantasy she'd once harboured? Of him saying he loved her and wanted to spend his life with her?

Surely she was stronger than that.

Arden pushed by him to pace the room, passing the exquisitely polished dining table with its crystal glasses, silverware and fine porcelain.

A table fit for a king. A king who'd planned to marry a princess. If anything was needed to highlight the differences between them that was it.

'What about your fiancée?' She swung to face him. Even from the far side of the room he was too close.

'I was never engaged. The betrothal wasn't finalised.'

Something in his voice told her he glossed over a difficult situation. Or maybe it was the hard line of his jaw. She could only guess at the diplomatic furore caused by those press reports.

'You don't just call off a royal marriage.'

'You expect me to wed Princess Ghizlan when I've discovered you're the mother of my son?' He grew before her eyes, his face taking on an implaable expression that made her think uneasily of his desert warrior heritage.

'I've been the mother of your son for years.' She folded her arms. 'We've survived quite well without you.'

It was the wrong thing to say. She knew it as soon as the words spilled out. The gleam in his eyes turned positively dangerous.

'I've been robbed of three years of my son's life.' He spoke quietly yet the lethal precision of those words sent her nerves into jangling alarm. 'I won't be robbed of more.'

'*I* didn't rob you of anything!' Her voice was overloud.

'Perhaps not.' She opened her mouth to speak again but the thoughtful, patient man who'd put Dawud's needs first all day had disappeared, replaced by a forbidding figure whose aggressive stance spoke of steely resolve. 'But the fact remains he's mine.'

'And mine!' Arden shot forward a step.

'Precisely. You said yourself it's best if a child has a positive relationship with both parents. Marriage will ensure that.'

'Marriage isn't required.' Arden stifled hollow laughter that she was rejecting him. Once the idea of marrying this man would have been a fantasy come true.

Because once she'd loved him with all the desperate, optimistic yearning of her young, innocent heart. She'd been drawn not just by his looks and charisma but by the way he *noticed* her. Shakil had made her feel special, as if she wasn't ordinary but remarkable. He'd shared new experiences with her, laughed with her, worked to please her with a generosity and charm that had seduced her completely. Now she realised she'd never really known him.

He tilted his head as if assessing her.

What did he see? An ordinary—too ordinary— young woman. Arden wasn't in the same league as Princess Ghizlan—beautiful, gracious and glamorous. Arden was a working class mum. She'd never owned a couture dress or mixed with the rich and famous.

Nor was she beautiful. Beneath the bright but untameable hair lurked an ordinary face, a short nose and mouth that, while well shaped, wasn't wide enough for current tastes. She juggled work and motherhood, was more at home singing nursery rhymes and cooking eggs with toast soldiers than dining in an elegant room like this.

'You're not thinking straight.' His jet eyebrows lifted and his eyes narrowed to gleaming slits, but Arden refused to be intimidated. 'This is a knee-jerk reaction. When you consider you'll realise the idea of us marrying is...'

'Logical? Long overdue? The best thing for Dawud?'

Arden shoved her hands on her hips, whipping

up outrage. 'I was thinking more ludicrous, unnecessary and painful.'

'You think marriage to me would be painful?'

Arden couldn't tell if it was shock or fury tightening his face but he morphed from broodingly aggressive to fearsome in the blink of an eye. Idris looked like a marauder planning a raid on some unprotected outpost.

A shiver ripped through her but she stood her ground. 'You'd find it painful. I'm not cut out to be a royal wife.'

And it would be painful for her, living a parody of the life she'd once imagined with the man she'd loved.

A slashing gesture, like the downward slice of a sword, dismissed her argument. 'You can learn.'

'I'm not interested in learning.' Why couldn't he see they were mismatched?

He stepped forward, not stopping till she felt his warm breath on her upturned face. Arden swallowed as a frisson of fear skated down her backbone.

'It may have escaped your notice, Arden.' He lingered on her name and the frisson became something else. Something that made a mockery of her antipathy. 'But it doesn't matter what you're interested in. What you and I want no longer counts. What matters is what's best for Dawud.'

Stupidly, her breath caught. He'd touched a

nerve. She'd do anything for her son, anything to ensure he had a bright, stable, happy future.

Except what Idris suggested was a recipe for disaster.

She folded her arms. 'Dawud doesn't need us to be married. It's far better if he has parents on friendly terms than ones making each other miserable because they married the wrong person.'

'Who do you want to marry?' It was out like a shot. 'My cousin?'

Arden backed a step and found her way blocked by a chair. 'No! Hamid is a friend, that's all.'

'Then who do you want to marry?' Idris stalked closer and Arden wondered how she'd ever considered him easy-going.

'No one. I was speaking in general terms. But that does raise the question of love.'

'Love?' He said it as if it was an alien concept.

'Of course.' Was he being deliberately difficult? 'If one of us fell in love with someone later…'

Idris shook his head. 'There's no danger of me falling in love with anyone else.'

For a split second the old Arden, the one she thought she'd left behind years ago, waited for him to declare he'd fallen for her all those years ago on Santorini.

It couldn't be true. That dream was ancient history. Yet her voice was husky. 'Why not?'

'I've never been in love and nor will I be. No one in my family marries for love.' He shrugged.

'We're renowned for being impervious to romance. Call it an inherited failing.'

'I see.' Stupid to feel disappointment. She'd known she'd only been a holiday fling. She'd long ago acknowledged her feelings for him were the product of girlish romanticism in the face of her first real crush.

'Unless you're afraid *you'll* fall in love?'

Arden's laugh was short and cynical. 'Definitely not.' The reality of becoming a single mother a week before her twenty-first birthday had shredded her romantic fantasies, even if seeing Idris again evoked shadowy memories of what she'd called love. She was too tired just getting through each day to think about romance.

'Good. Then that's not a problem.'

Arden shook her head. 'But there are plenty more.'

'Such as?'

Was he serious? The whole idea was laughable.

'Your people won't accept me as Queen.'

'My people will accept any woman I marry.' It was said with a conviction that told her it was the absolute truth.

'I couldn't accept the restrictions of being a woman in your country. Your traditions are different to mine.'

That pulled him up short. Arden watched his brow crinkle.

'It's true our traditions aren't the same,' he said

slowly, 'but change is happening. My country is very different to the way it was four years ago. Besides, as my wife, you'd be able to model change for other women, to lead the way.'

'Princess Ghizlan would do that far better.'

He shook his head, his lips flattening. 'How many times do I have to tell you she's out of the picture? I can't ask her to marry me in the face of this scandal. The only decent thing I can do, for everyone, is marry you.'

That put her in her place. She was nothing but an albatross around his neck.

She heaved in a deep breath. 'I'm sorry for the trouble the news has caused. To *all* of us. My life's not going to be easy either, at least for a while. But it's not my fault. Nor do I think jumping into marriage is a solution. All I want is what's best for Dawud.'

'At last we agree on something.'

His words gave her hope. Maybe he could be persuaded. She hadn't exactly been tactful in rejecting his proposal. If you could call his statement that they'd marry a proposal!

Arden lifted her lips in a small, conciliatory smile. 'You're right. That's a starting point, isn't it?'

He gave no answering smile and Arden wondered how often people argued with the Sheikh of Zahrat. Was he so used to having his own way he couldn't concede there were other options?

'Look. Why don't we sit down and discuss some possibilities?'

To her relief he stepped back, allowing her to slip into her vacated seat. Just in time. Stress and weariness had taken their toll. Her legs shook as if she'd run all the way to the top of St Paul's Cathedral.

Idris settled beside her. 'You were saying?'

'Well…' She slid a fork across the tablecloth, watching grooves appear then disappear in the fine linen. 'Perhaps he could spend part of the year with you.'

Just saying it stabbed pain through her chest. She couldn't imagine a day without Dawud. Her breath snared in an audible hiss.

But she had to be realistic. Dawud should have a chance to know his father.

'As a part-time prince, you mean? Living sometimes in my palace and sometimes in your basement flat?'

Arden's head jerked up. His voice was cool, almost detached, but surely that was anger she heard?

'It makes more sense than pretending the three of us can be the perfect family.'

'I'm not asking for perfection, Arden.'

She bit down her retort that he hadn't *asked* anything. But bickering would get them nowhere. She had to put aside resentment and fear and think of what was best for Dawud. Even if being with Idris made her feel trapped. 'Sharing him is a workable compromise.'

'You really think Dawud can go back to the life he used to lead now I know he's mine?'

Arden stiffened. The heavy silver fork thudded to the table. She worked hard to provide for her boy. 'Why not? A dose of working class reality to compare with palace life might be a good thing.'

Idris shook his head. 'You misunderstand. The damage is done now the world knows Dawud is my son. It's my duty, as well as my wish, to have him live with me. If I don't I'd be remiss and I'd be thought weak by my people. It would be an insult to you too, if I didn't marry you. And an insult to Ghizlan if I rejected her then didn't marry the mother of my son.'

Arden gritted her teeth. 'I'm a person in my own right.' She didn't care what his people or his Princess thought. All she cared about was Dawud.

'You would let your personal preferences stand in the way of Dawud's happiness and safety?'

'You're exaggerating. I've cared for him perfectly well up till now.'

'That was before.' A large hand covered hers, clamping it to the table. She was surprised how reassuring that touch felt. 'You've only had one day's taste of what the press can do. Do you want to put Dawud through that again and again?'

A chill invaded her bones. 'Surely once the novelty wears off...'

'Arden, this won't go away. Ever. Whenever there's an item of news about my country, or a slow media day, or a significant event for you or Dawud—a birthday, his first day at school, even weekend sports—the press will be there, snapping candid photos. They'll rehash the story—the difference between my life in the palace and his in London. Every step he takes will be pored over, particularly since he's so photogenic. Every decision you make as a mother will be scrutinised and judged.'

She was almost grateful for the warmth of his hand as her skin crawled at the picture he painted.

'Dawud won't have anywhere to hide. He'll be hounded, a freak for the press to exploit.'

Arden ripped her hand away and pressed it to her pounding chest. 'Dawud isn't a freak!'

'Of course not. He's a perfectly normal little boy.' Idris's voice curled comfortingly around her. 'I want him to stay that way.'

'By making him live in a palace!'

Idris's chuckle was rich and far too appealing. It reminded her of Shakil, the man who could make her heart turn over with just a smile. 'You make it sound like a prison. Believe me, Dawud can live a more normal life there than in London. In Zahrat I can protect you both.'

Arden swallowed a clot of apprehension. It was too extreme to contemplate. Yet in her heart of hearts she knew Idris was right. She and Dawud couldn't go back.

A great shudder racked her.

'I suppose we could try living in Zahrat, if you helped find us a house.' Could she work there? Did they even have florists? She put her hand to her temple, where a dull thudding headache had taken root.

'You would live in the palace. As my wife. It's the only sensible option. Together we can give him a stable home, no end-of-week handovers and complicated custody.' Idris didn't look aggressive now, just coolly composed. As if he knew he held all the aces.

Arden slumped in her seat. She felt cornered, her mind whirling fruitlessly as she sought alternatives to the one Idris presented.

'This is about Dawud,' he murmured. 'About what's best for our boy.'

Our boy. Not his son, or her son. *Our boy.*

That one small phrase bridged the gaping chasm between them. It made her feel less alone.

That shouldn't matter. She was used to shouldering responsibility. Yet there was a disarming allure to the idea of sharing this load.

'I need to think.' She slid her hand out from beneath his. 'I need time.'

'Of course. I'll come for your decision at nine tomorrow morning.'

* * *

At four the next afternoon, and after a night of soul-searching, Arden became betrothed to Idris, Sheikh of Zahrat in front of a throng of witnesses.

She'd planned to reject him. The idea of tying herself to the man who, accidentally or not, had left her floundering four years before, rankled. She wanted to walk away, defiant, independent and dismissive.

But she, more than most, understood what it was to be utterly alone and unprotected. If anything happened to her... No, Dawud had the right to grow up secure and loved, free from press intrusion, free to accept his birthright if he wished. And from all she'd been able to discover from the Internet, Idris would work as hard at being a good father as he did every other responsibility. He had a reputation for honest dealing and care for his subjects.

Yet her signature on the contract was shaky, like a child's just learning to write, because she trembled all over, her stomach twisting in knots. Beside her on his throne Idris signed with a slashing flourish that reflected complete ease.

No doubt he was used to signing important papers. But as she stared at the massive parchment with its gilt edging and beautiful decorative calligraphy border, Arden felt she'd signed her life away. Hers and her son's.

A chill clamped her neck and shoulders and her heart pounded so hard she was surprised no one heard it. She'd had no real choice, yet still she worried—

'Let me be the first to congratulate you.'

She looked up to see Princess Ghizlan. In an amber silk suit and a fortune in pearls around her throat, she looked every inch the glamorous, aristocratic princess. Everything Arden would never be, despite the costly outfit Idris had provided as an alternative to her ancient jeans.

Surprisingly the other woman's smile was warm and Arden felt grateful. She'd been alarmed when she'd spied the Princess amidst the serious men in the throne room. After all, she'd been all but jilted because of Arden.

'Thank you, Your—'

'Ghizlan, please.' She turned to Idris. 'Congratulations on your betrothal, Your Highness. I hope you'll both be very happy.'

There was nothing in her face or his to indicate anything between them but calm goodwill. No tension, no fraught looks. Were they superb actors, Arden wondered, or was it true the match between them had been nothing but a formality? Arden's head spun. This royal world she'd entered was confusing and unnatural.

'Thank you.' His voice was deep and grave, a reminder that this ceremony was about securing his son's future, not anything as joyous or natural as a love match. He hadn't smiled once today.

Because this is about duty and respectability. Nothing more.

Arden's heart gave another heavy thump, rising up against her throat.

'I wondered if I might steal you away to take some refreshment.'

Arden was on her feet instantly then paused, wavering. Was she supposed to sit beside Idris to accept congratulations? But he was getting up and, frankly, she'd had enough formality.

'That sounds lovely.' As she followed the other woman to the lavish buffet her stomach growled. She'd been too nervous to eat.

'I'm the same,' said Ghizlan softly. 'I don't eat before official engagements then I regret it. They go on far too long.'

Arden cast a sideways look at the statuesque woman now filling a fine porcelain plate with delicacies.

'You really don't mind about...me?' she blurted out, then silently cursed her crassness. This wasn't the time or place. But she was curious about this poised, beautiful woman who'd so nearly married Idris.

The Princess cut her a swift look. 'Let's go somewhere more comfortable.' She nodded to lounges in a corner Arden hadn't even seen.

All she'd noticed on entering the room was the

crowd and Idris, tall and unsmiling. Her pulse had tumbled out of kilter as she drank in his spare, handsome features. It horrified her that just looking at him left her breathless.

'Arden? I may call you Arden?'

'Of course... Ghizlan. I'm sorry, I'm a little distracted.' She sank into a seat, carefully holding her plate of delicious-smelling food.

'I'm not surprised. If you're not used to these formal ceremonies they can be daunting.' The other woman leaned close. 'The trick is to have something else to think of during the boring bits. I do my best planning then.'

A smile tugged Arden's lips and some of that horrible, wound-too-tight feeling in her stomach settled. 'It's good of you to be so nice to me. I didn't expect—I mean, thank you. I didn't mean—'

Ghizlan's lustrous kohl-lined eyes widened, then she laughed, the sound rich and appealing. Male heads turned.

'You're absolutely welcome. I suspect I'm going to like you very much.'

Arden plonked her plate on a table and leaned closer. 'I didn't mean it to come out that way.'

Ghizlan waved away her words. 'It's good to hear someone so frank. You'll understand once you're hemmed in by diplomats and courtiers. And you're right.' She paused. 'This is tough for all of us.'

'I'm truly sorry about that.'

'It's not your fault. None of us had a choice once the news came out about your boy.'

Arden searched the beautiful face for signs of hurt but read nothing. 'It must be especially difficult for you.'

Ghizlan looked away. 'A diplomatic storm, that's for sure. But it will pass. Our betrothal hadn't been formalised, and now, if you and I are seen together on friendly terms things will ease a little.'

Slowly Arden nodded. *That* was why Ghizlan was here. It wasn't simple goodwill behind this *tête-à-tête*. Disappointment stirred. 'I see. You think this—' her gesture encompassed the pair of them in the intimate cluster of seats '—will help stave off gossip?'

'Now *you're* offended. I'm sorry. I told Idris you mightn't want me here, but he assured me there was no sentimental attachment between you. Please forgive me.'

She made to rise but Arden's out-thrust hand stopped her. 'No, please.'

A roiling wave of emotion surged through her. Idris's words shouldn't hurt. They were true. Anything they'd once felt for each other was long dead. And what had Ghizlan done but try to ameliorate a disaster?

'I'm sorry.' Arden swallowed hard. 'I do appreciate you being here. It must have been difficult for you and it's nice to have another woman here.'

'I thought it might help. Plus it will take some

of the fuel from the fire if it looks like I'm in London to support you instead of being on approval for Idris.'

'On approval?'

Ghizlan's face took on that smooth, unruffled expression that Arden now realised masked other feelings. 'Our marriage was to build a bridge between our two countries that have feuded for generations. It was tied to a peace treaty and a trade agreement but still, we needed a little time in each other's company to...test the waters.'

Arden blinked as something hot and jagged, something almost like jealousy, bit into her. But she jammed a stop on her imagination before she could wonder how far *testing the waters* went.

'There'll be hell to pay when I return home but meanwhile supporting you helps us both by deflecting the worst of the gossip.'

Arden looked into that beautiful face, so still and poised, and realised how much courage it took for the other woman to be here, smiling as if her hopes of marriage hadn't been dashed so scandalously. If she...*cared* for Idris...

To her amazement, fellow feeling rose. She'd loved and lost him once and it had soured her on the idea of love ever since. But she'd never forgotten the pain. It still sideswiped her when she least expected it.

'I like your thinking, Ghizlan.' Arden hesitated then plunged on. 'Maybe you could advise me a little about what to expect? I know nothing about protocol and ceremony, or even what I should wear.'

She looked down at the pretty pale blue dress that shimmered under the brilliant lights. It had appeared in her room this morning and she'd accepted it gratefully rather than face this ceremony in old denims.

If she let herself dwell on how unprepared she was, she'd hide away and never come out. Or work herself into a fury at how she was being railroaded. But it was too late for second thoughts.

'You like the dress?'

'It's gorgeous. But I have no experience in buying expensive clothes and I have no idea what's required for...' Arden's words faded as she saw the smile on the other woman's face. '*You* picked this?'

Ghizlan shrugged. 'Just gave a couple of suggestions. I thought, given how quickly this all happened you mightn't have anything suitable for today.'

Arden blinked as gratitude welled. 'You really are a nice woman, aren't you?'

Before she could feel self-conscious about blurting out her thoughts again, Ghizlan gave a delighted laugh.

Idris followed the muted sound of laughter to see both women with their heads together. One dark, one golden, both beautiful, his rejected bride and his affianced bride.

His belly tightened at the thought of the frantic work he had still to do to salvage something from the debacle caused by Arden and Dawud. Relations with Ghizlan's royal father were in tatters, as were the treaties they'd negotiated. Conservative elements in his own country were up in arms about his illegitimate son and his plans to marry an Englishwoman. Yet what alternative did he have?

Any other course would be ruinous.

Any other course would deprive him of his son and make Dawud an object of ridicule and gossip.

Any other course would deprive him of Arden.

He watched her lean in to talk with Ghizlan. The movement tugged her silk dress tight, outlining that slim, delicious figure he'd fantasised about all night.

With half an ear he listened to the conversation around him, the first steps in building a new rapport with representatives of Ghizlan's father. Yet his attention was fixed on Arden. The woman he would marry.

For the first time since he'd agreed to consider taking a bride, he felt a sharp tug of eagerness.

Arden might be trouble on two beautiful, sexy legs. She had no pedigree, no dowry or influence in his region. Worse, she had no training for a royal role, no knowledge of diplomacy or the arcane ceremonies and rituals which still persisted at court.

Yet she was the mother of his son and for that alone would be accorded respect.

Except that wasn't the only reason he would marry her, was it? Last night he'd confronted the uncomfortable truth that he couldn't in all honesty marry Ghizlan when it was Arden he wanted in his bed.

Want was such a weak word for the hunger simmering within him. It might be just sex, but it felt alarmingly like a compulsion. Like the weakness all the men of his family shared, a weakness he'd thought he'd put aside when he took on the sheikhdom.

He must learn to conquer this weakness or master it. He intended to approach this marriage like any other contract. With a cool head and in total control.

CHAPTER SIX

'AN AIR-CONDITIONED LIMOUSINE will drive you and your son to the palace, Ms Wills.' Ashar, the Sheikh's aide, smiled reassuringly from the seat beside her on the plane. 'It's a short drive and it won't be long before you're settling into your rooms to rest.'

'Thank you.' A rest sounded wonderful. Even here in the comfort of Idris's private jet Arden hadn't been able to relax.

Perhaps because she wasn't used to people waiting on her. Misha, their temporary nanny, had taken Dawud to another cabin in the luxurious aircraft so Arden didn't have the distraction of a toddler who'd crush her new designer suit. Yet instead of revelling in the luxury of some quiet time Arden felt deprived. Of course she could have gone to him, but deep down she realised her stress wasn't about Dawud, it was about her fears for the future.

What had she done, agreeing to leave London and marry Idris? Could she marry him and trust him to do what was best for Dawud?

Logic reminded her Idris wasn't the carefree, careless young man who'd left her bereft and struggling. She'd seen the change in him. Yet she couldn't stifle unease.

Everything had happened so fast, the betrothal ceremony, the blur of new faces as Idris's personal staff were introduced. The shopping trip with Ghizlan to a famous couturier who'd opened his doors just for them while stony-faced security men kept the press at a distance.

Resigning from her job by phone had been a surreal experience. Her boss had read about her 'adventure' and had been agog for news. Arden was left with the unsettling suspicion she'd be more valuable to the business now she was an almost-VIP and potential drawcard than ever before. As for closing up the flat—it had been done for her. Idris had spoken to Hamid before she could, explaining she wouldn't be returning.

Of everything that had happened in the last few days, that was the worst. It felt as if her life had been ripped away. She'd poured in hours of work and what little cash she had, turning it into a warm, bright home, full of treasured memories.

It didn't matter that everything was done efficiently and with exquisite politeness by the royal staff. Beneath every courteous query about her preferences lay a stark, terrifying truth.

She had no choice in anything that mattered

now. She'd agreed to marry Dawud's father and their lives would be dominated by that from now on.

'I'm sorry.' She blinked and focused on the royal aide. 'You were saying?'

'I asked if you'd like some water or anything else. You look pale and we're about to land. If you're ill…?'

Arden shook her head. 'I'm okay, thanks. Just tired.'

'Then I'll leave you alone for now.' Ashar nodded and melted away.

Arden's lips twisted. Wasn't that the perfect indicator of what this royal marriage would be like? It wasn't her soon-to-be husband asking about her well-being. Idris had excused himself as soon as they boarded and headed into a study off the main cabin. She'd barely seen him since she'd agreed to marry him. It was left to his ever-watchful staff to be concerned for her.

Arden straightened her shoulders. She didn't need their concern. She could do this. She *had* to do this.

No matter how tough, no matter how challenging her new life, she'd face it like she'd faced everything else life threw at her.

After a lifetime solo, one important thing had changed. She was no longer alone. She had Dawud. He was more precious to her than anything, even phantom memories of first love and heartbreak.

She did this for her son.

Arden turned to look out of the window, staring at the misty blue mountains that rose in the distance, jagged and forbidding. Below her a broad, tawny plain sprawled to the coast where white sand edged a turquoise sea.

Zahrat. Legendary for its fiercely independent people and its arid vastness of desert and rugged mountains.

Despite her determination to be strong, Arden couldn't repress a fervent wish that she and Dawud were safely back in London, leading their familiar, ordinary lives.

From astride his horse Idris surveyed the people lining the streets that wound through the capital. Every man, woman and child, it seemed, had come out to see their Sheikh make his traditional entry to the city.

And to see his son, and the Englishwoman who'd soon be their Sheikha.

As decreed by custom, there was no applause, no shouting, merely bowed heads as he passed. Yet that didn't stop the crowd craning for a view of the vehicle following him, the car carrying Arden and Dawud.

He'd wondered how the news of his ready-made family would be taken. Not that anything would deter him from his duty to marry.

His people were proud and traditional. No doubt

the older, more conservative ones would frown about a foreign bride. Yet he noticed a few silken banners, a customary sign of rejoicing, flying in the street. Turquoise for the sea that bordered Zahrat and scarlet for the desert at sunset, or, as popular belief had it, for the blood of their enemies, shed whenever the Zahrati defended their land.

Idris was musing on this sign of welcome when the Captain of the Royal Guard rode close.

'Highness. The car. It's stopped.'

Instantly alert, Idris whipped around, pulling his horse to a halt.

There was no sign of a problem yet his heartbeat quickened, his body tense, ready for action as he scanned the street for signs of an ambush. Security was a necessity these days, yet in his homeland Idris had always felt his bodyguard was more to satisfy tradition than because of any threat.

But if anyone were to threaten Dawud and Arden—

The rear door of the limousine opened and she emerged, the afternoon sun turning her hair to spun rose gold. The quiet crowd seemed to still completely. The silence grew complete so the thud of his horse's hooves as it pranced towards the car filled the void. That and the rough pulse of blood in his ears.

What was she doing? No stop had been scheduled. Was she ill? Was his son ill?

Idris vaulted from his horse, thrusting the reins

into the hand of a nearby guard, then slammed to a halt.

That was why the cavalcade had stopped?

Arden crossed to the side of the street where the onlookers crowded in the shade of an ancient shop awning. Near the front of the packed group one single person had ignored tradition. A girl, no more than six or seven by the look of her skinny frame. She sat in a wheelchair, gripping a straggly bouquet of flowers, her eyes huge as Arden approached.

In her slim-fitting straw-coloured suit that gleamed subtly under the fierce sun, Arden probably looked like a creature from another world to the girl.

The sight of Arden, cool and sophisticated with her high heels and her hair up, had stolen his breath when he'd seen her earlier. The air had punched from his lungs as desire surged, as fresh and strong as it had been years ago. Desire and admiration and something else, some emotion that was tangled up in the fact she'd borne his child. *His responsibility to protect. His.*

His visceral reaction had been possessiveness. The desire to claim her, and with far more than words, had sent him into retreat. He'd taken a separate vehicle to the airport and on the plane had immersed himself in work. Keeping his distance meant keeping control.

Arden stopped before the girl and crouched

down, saying something he couldn't make out. He strode across, his steps decisive on the ancient cobbles.

The girl whispered something, shyly smiling, and held out the flowers which, he saw now, were no more than a collection of wildflowers such as grew in the rare fertile areas near the city. One of them, yellow as the sun, looked like a dandelion.

But Arden held them carefully, as if they were the most precious bouquet.

'*Shukran jazīlan,* Leila.'

The little girl's face lit up and from the clustering crowd murmurs rose.

Idris stopped, stunned. Arden spoke his language? He listened, amazed, as she went on, haltingly but competently, to ask where the girl lived.

The conversation was short, for soon the child noticed him and grew too shy to speak.

Idris repressed a frown. The girl's reaction wasn't surprising. People didn't address the royal Sheikh unless invited, yet he couldn't help but feel like a big, black thundercloud, blotting out the sun and marring their rapport. Especially when Arden looked over her shoulder, her mouth compressing when she saw him.

He didn't want her to look at him like that. He wanted her to look at him with the dazed longing he'd seen too briefly the day he'd kissed her at her front door. Or, better yet, with that expression of awe and bliss he remembered from years ago, when she'd been eager for him, especially in bed.

His thoughts horrified. Here, on the main street of his capital, under the gaze of thousands of his subjects, he was fretting over a woman. He was caught in a morass of political and diplomatic difficulties because of the current scandal—every waking moment he was busy negotiating a minefield of trouble and trying to salvage the peace treaty—and he let himself be distracted.

Arden stood and turned, her expression this time blank. Which, absurdly, made Idris clamp his jaw tighter as he took her arm and escorted her to the car.

She felt surprisingly fragile beneath the fine fabric of her new clothes, making him even more aware of the imbalance of power between them. He told himself they were both victims of circumstance. He did only what he must for the sake of his child and his country. But he disliked the reminder of Arden's fragility, the fact she'd given up everything she knew to come here, an unwilling bride.

He paused, breathing deep, searching for the sense of calm and control that had eluded him since Arden had burst back into his life.

With careful courtesy he helped her into the car, gave a few instructions to waiting staff, then stalked around the car and got in.

* * *

Arden's eyes widened as Idris took the far corner of the back seat. Even with Dawud's child seat between them Idris dominated the rear of the huge limo.

He'd looked larger than life astride his gleaming horse and to her dismay her heart had done crazy flip flops as she watched him through the windscreen. She'd never seen him in traditional dress and was amazed how the horseman's outfit with loose trousers tucked into long boots, a white headdress and light cloak had turned the most attractive man she'd ever seen into the stuff of pure fantasy.

The fantasy had died when she'd turned to find him looming over her like a disgruntled bear. He couldn't have made it clearer that she'd broken some taboo by getting out of the car and talking to little Leila.

Arden refused to apologise. Her heart had caught at the sight of the little girl and that one tiny token of welcome after kilometres of staring, silent, obviously disapproving people.

'Are you going to tell me off now or wait till we get to the palace?' She glanced at the closed window shutting them off from the driver and bodyguard in the front.

'Tell you off?' His words were abrupt, as if jerked from him.

Arden rolled her eyes and turned. He looked as

forbidding as he had out on the street but stupidly some weak, utterly female part of her found him compellingly handsome. Her gaze dropped to his sculpted lips, now in a flat line, and she had the crazy impulse to lean over and kiss him till his pent-up fury disappeared.

That was one impulse she would *not* give in to!

She opened her mouth to speak but a sound stopped her. She whipped her head around to stare at the people crowding the street. The noise, a high-pitched, rhythmic trill, swelled, surrounding them, making the hairs on her arms prickle upright.

'What's that?' Reflexively one arm shot protectively across the front of the seat where Dawud slept.

'It's all right. It's nothing to worry about.' Idris's deep voice reassured. 'Quite the opposite. It's a sign of approval.'

'Approval?' Her head jerked around as the car slid forward.

Idris's lips quirked at one corner. Not quite a smile but the closest she'd seen to one in days, and even that had been directed at Dawud, not her.

'Don't look so worried. Approval of you.'

'Me?' She turned back to look out of the window, watching the faces slide by. 'Why? Because I spoke to that little girl? Surely it's not such a big deal.' In the UK it wasn't unusual for VIPs to talk with people who'd waited patiently to see them.

Besides, Arden was a long way from being a VIP. She felt like an imposter in this procession.

'It *is* a big deal in Zahrat. Where the royal family is concerned tradition is slow to change. And tradition has it that when the Sheikh enters the city his people will greet him in silence, bowing to show their loyalty.'

Arden's heart sank. She hadn't even arrived at the palace and already she'd broken some important rule.

'So I shouldn't have stopped and got out?' She frowned. 'Leila won't get into trouble, will she? I spoke to her before she spoke to me, you know.'

He shook his head, that elusive hint of a smile rippling further along his mouth. She felt an answering pang deep inside. Once his smile had made her glow all over, when she'd believed he loved her.

'Far from it. She'll be the centre of attention. She'll probably dine out on the story when she's old and grey.'

'So it's just me who's broken the unwritten law.'

'More a guideline than a law.' Lustrous dark eyes held hers and Arden felt her heart thump against her ribcage. 'And I told you, that's approval you hear. You'll hear it again the day we celebrate our wedding.'

She'd got this far by not thinking about their marriage. It was a travesty of all she held dear. To marry not for love but for show went against all the hopes she'd once cherished.

'They were impressed too that you spoke our language.' He paused. '*I* was impressed. Why didn't you tell me?'

'Why should I? Clearly it made no difference to my suitability as your wife.' Was it imagination or did she truly taste bitterness on the word *wife*? 'Besides, I don't really speak it. I started learning but didn't get far. I was too busy with Dawud and work.' She thought grimly how those words glossed over her constant exhaustion as she'd struggled to provide for her son. Lucky she was good at her job so her boss had been understanding. 'I only know some very basic phrases but Hamid helped me practice the pronunciation.'

Idris's eyebrows slanted down in what could only be described as a scowl. What was his problem? That she only knew a few phrases after all? Or was it something to do with Hamid? Surely he wasn't still convinced she and Hamid were lovers? He'd spoken to his cousin. He must know now that wasn't true, even if Hamid had begun to see their relationship leading further than she wanted it to go.

'Nevertheless, it's a valuable bonus that you know as much as you do, and that you've demonstrated it to my people. That's one more thing in your favour when it comes to them accepting this marriage.'

'In addition to my son, you mean?'

Idris had made it clear their relationship, if you could call it that, was a necessary evil.

'*Our* son, Arden.'

For long seconds he held her gaze, till she felt heat rise in her cheeks and turned away. It was fantasy to imagine she read something intimate in those black velvet eyes.

The road was rising and above the rooftops a citadel rose, amber in the sunlight, on sheer cliffs. A massive palace grew there, apparently out of the very rock. Its roof glittered, dazzling her eyes even from this distance.

Idris must have followed her gaze.

'The Palace of Gold,' he murmured. 'Your new home.'

CHAPTER SEVEN

ARDEN HAD BEEN dumbfounded by the palace when she'd seen it from the limousine. But the interior was even more stunning. The older parts of the building featured walls studded with semiprecious jewels, while the modernised sections were unlike anything she'd ever seen.

She knew Idris was a man with a deeply sensual side but she was shocked at the luxury of his home. Until Ashar, her guide when Idris excused himself and disappeared down another corridor, mentioned it had been Idris's uncle, the previous Sheikh, who'd lavishly updated the royal accommodation.

Arden's suite was vast, comprising a bedroom for Dawud with a bathroom and playroom that linked to accommodation for the nanny. For Arden there was a sitting room, study and bedroom. The bedroom had three walls of pale sea-green silk which on one side hid a walk-in wardrobe and a bathroom almost as big as her old flat.

Scallop-edged arched windows gave an unrivalled view of the city and the coast beyond. Her bed, the biggest she'd ever seen, sat on a raised platform with ornamental drapes of silver tissue pulled back from the head. Exquisite raised plasterwork on the wall behind it gave the impression of a vast silvery tree with delicate curling shoots and leaves inlaid with mother-of-pearl.

She couldn't begin to imagine how many hours of craftsmanship had gone into decorating the room, much less the cost.

As for sleeping here…

Arden shook her head. She'd feel like an imposter, curled up in that vast luxurious bed. The room was a breathtaking fantasy, designed for a princess.

She looked down at the silver-embroidered bedspread, noticing intricately stitched figures of horsemen in procession, banners streaming, riding across the spread. Horsemen with the proud warrior demeanour of Idris as he'd sat astride his stallion today. Until she'd stopped the cavalcade to talk with Leila.

Arden stared at her hand on the fine embroidery. Pale skin instead of the lovely golden colour of the locals and of Princess Ghizlan. Short, sensible nails. Hands that were nimble and strong after years working as a florist, wiring bouquets, lifting heavy buckets of water, snipping and arranging and making deliveries. *Not* the delicate, pampered hands of a princess, despite her recent manicure.

What on earth was she doing here?

Arden's knees gave way and she collapsed onto the edge of the mattress, chest tight and breath unsteady.

Just as well she'd left Dawud in his playroom under Misha's watchful eye while she explored the suite. Arden didn't want him to see her anything but calm. She couldn't afford to let her doubts and fears mar his acceptance of their new surroundings. Not if they were to stay here.

Anxiety gnawed at her belly.

She firmed her lips. She'd already faced this doubt and decided she was doing the right thing for Dawud. Yet that didn't stop the horrible sensation of being trapped. Losing control of her future scared her, as much as the unwanted emotions Idris stirred. The longing for what could never be. What she needed now was something familiar, something normal. Someone on her side.

Hamid. She hadn't spoken to him since the night of the embassy reception. The night her life went off the rails.

Arden reached for her phone, then hesitated. She'd wanted to talk with Hamid about the change in him—from friend to would-be lover. But so much had happened that she hadn't picked up the phone. Now, thanks to Idris, Hamid knew she was betrothed to his cousin.

She drew in a slow breath. This wouldn't be easy. But no matter what false hopes Hamid had begun to harbour, he'd been a good friend when she needed him and she owed him an explanation. She'd never told him who Dawud's father was, because by then she'd given up trying to find him, believing Shakil had unceremoniously duped and dumped her. Hamid must be reeling too.

She punched in his number and lifted the phone.

Idris found her in the bedroom. She still wore the pale gold suit that emphasised her slenderness, but she'd kicked off her shoes. The sight of her bare feet on the intricate mosaic floor conjured images of the rest of her naked. Naked and willing in his bed. Once her fresh enthusiasm, sweet honesty and sexy body had made her more alluring than any woman he'd known. It seemed that hadn't changed.

His heart gave a now familiar thump—a symptom of the weakness he hadn't been able to eradicate. Even now when, because of her, he faced a diplomatic nightmare in his homeland and more especially with their regional neighbours.

Relations with Ghizlan's country had been tinder-dry for generations and the prospect of a dynastic marriage to seal their new-found peace was a huge win for his people's well-being. Now that was in tatters.

He should be dealing with the fallout, ensuring peace and prosperity, especially now he had a family to care for as well as a nation. Instead he'd taken a break from crisis talks that would go on all night to check on Arden. Idris raised a hand to knock but let it fall as she spoke.

'I understand, Hamid.' She leaned against the window frame, her posture defeated—head bowed and shoulders slumped. 'Of course.' She swiped at her cheek. 'Goodbye, then.'

The sight of her dejection hit Idris a hammer blow. There was a crammed full feeling in his chest, the suspicion of an ache there at odds with the fire of anger in his belly. Was she really so cut up about leaving Hamid? Had she been in love with him?

Idris considered himself a civilised man, far removed from the tyrants who'd ruled this country long ago. Yet at the moment he'd happily have slammed his fist into his cousin before throwing him into a dungeon.

He stepped into the room, the riding boots he still wore loud on the fine tiles.

Arden's head whipped up and he had a swift impression of tear-glazed eyes and burning cheeks before she pivoted away to place her phone on a bedside table.

When she turned back her colour was high but she was completely composed.

'I'd prefer you to knock before coming into my room.' She folded her arms. Did she know how provocative she looked? Her hair was coming down in sensual waves around her shoulders and her touch-me-not air was an incitement to tip her back onto the bed and put an end to the pretence she didn't want him as he wanted her.

Except she'd been crying over his cousin. The thought was an icy douche to desire.

'You'll need to get used to my presence in the suite.' When she opened her mouth he continued. 'I intend to see my son regularly and establish a relationship with him. I've got three years to catch up on, remember?'

Slowly Arden nodded. 'Of course.' Her voice was croaky. 'But not in my bedroom.'

Idris was tempted to inform her this was the royal bedroom, to be shared by the Sheikh and Sheikha. But she looked so damnably vulnerable with her stiff spine and sad eyes. It made him feel, yet again, that *he* were in the wrong. When he was the one putting things right!

Besides, he'd promised himself he'd keep out of Arden's bed. There was enough scandal already. He would honour tradition and his bride-to-be by keeping his distance temporarily.

'Then come into the sitting room. We need to talk.'

Arden watched him disappear with a swish of his long cloak from spectacular shoulders and fought the squiggle of feminine heat swirling through her.

Would it always be this way? Would she always go weak at the knees around Idris?

She flattened her lips and told herself it was just

memory—the fact he'd been her first and only lover. In time she'd look at him and feel nothing.

The enormity of that lie almost undid her. If anything, her yearning for the warmth they'd once shared, the crazy but potent sense of belonging, was stronger than in all the years since they'd parted.

She didn't want to face him. But she had no choice.

He stood near the window, feet wide, hands on hips, face set in stern lines. He looked as if he ruled everything he surveyed.

Arden bit down rueful laughter, realising it was true. He *did* rule it all.

'You wanted to talk?' She sank onto a chair, repressing a flutter of foreboding. His mouth looked stern, as if something displeased him.

That would be her. Already defying protocol on her first day as well as upsetting his plans for a grand marriage.

The idea of becoming Sheikha was as appealing as walking a tightrope. She hated the certainty she'd fail ignominiously.

'I do. We need to set some ground rules.'

'Ground rules?' Her brow puckered.

His wide shoulders lifted. 'We've had no discussion about our expectations of each other.'

Arden sank back. 'You mean like not coming into my room uninvited?'

His lips flattened but he nodded. 'That sort of thing.'

Arden racked her tired brain. This wasn't the best time to talk, when she was exhausted and stressed. But she owed it to herself and Dawud to take the opportunity.

'I want an equal say in all decisions affecting Dawud, his education and how he lives.'

Idris's black eyebrows slanted down. 'There are traditions around how a crown prince is raised.'

'And I'll try to respect as many of those as I can. But I insist on the right to decide, with you.' It was an enormous concession. She'd always made every decision for her son. Learning to share would be tough—relinquishing any control over him scared her. But she'd agreed living here was best for Dawud. Now, reluctantly, she had to make that work, no matter the personal sacrifices, like pretending to be something she wasn't and consulting Idris on important issues.

'If I don't like the traditional ways, I expect full consultation. I expect us to negotiate an agreed solution. And I need that agreement in writing.' Arden laced her fingers tightly. Idris had the weight of royal authority but she refused to budge. She couldn't gamble on Dawud's well-being. 'If you can't agree to that the deal is off.'

Those expressive eyebrows rose. 'You'd try to back out of the marriage?'

Arden lifted her chin. 'Not *try*. I *would*. I'm accepting your terms by coming to live here, and by agreeing to marry. But I won't give up the right to decide what's best for my son.'

For long seconds Idris surveyed her silently, then abruptly he nodded. 'That's fair. I agree.'

Arden sank back, her heart racing. She'd been prepared for a fight.

'What else?'

What else mattered as much as her son?

'I'll try not to flout too many traditions in Zahrat, but I'd prefer to wear my own clothes, western clothes, most of the time. I wouldn't be comfortable wearing a veil.'

His sculpted lips lifted at the corners. 'You may not have noticed, but veils are optional. A lot of women, at least in the cities, opt for western dress. Zahrat is traditional in many ways but very few would expect a European woman to dress in Zahrati costume.' He paused. 'Anything more?'

There were probably lots of things but that was all she could think of at the moment. Except for one thing.

'Even though this isn't an ordinary marriage, I'd prefer it if you kept any…liaisons private. I don't want to know about them and I don't want Dawud to hear about them when he's older.' It would be enough trying to make this marriage of convenience work without Idris flaunting his lovers. The idea of those faceless, but no doubt gorgeous, women made her feel nauseous.

'My liaisons?' The hint of a smile vanished from his face.

'Your lovers.' She dragged in a tight breath. 'I'd appreciate you being discreet.'

His nostrils flared as if he repressed annoyance, but he gave a curt nod. 'Agreed.'

Arden tried to feel relieved but instead felt absurdly wobbly. Her husband-to-be had just promised to keep his lovers out of sight. It wasn't as if this were a love match. It was a paper marriage for purely practical reasons, but it seemed plain wrong to go into it making arrangements for other women to share her husband's bed.

Especially when, to her dismay, he still made her crave intimacies she'd never shared with anyone but him. Not just sex but the warm feeling of being appreciated, being special.

'Arden?'

'Sorry?'

'I asked if there was anything else.'

She shook her head. 'That's all I can think of at the moment. Now, if you'll excuse me...' She made to get up from her seat.

'Not so fast. You haven't heard my expectations.' Gleaming eyes held hers and suddenly Arden found herself breathless.

'It's not enough that I move here and agree to marry you? I'm the one making all the concessions.' Her voice was strident, masking nerves.

'Believe it or not, we're both making compromises, Arden.' He said no more but she knew he was thinking of Princess Ghizlan, beautiful, charming, no doubt with a pedigree a mile long and an innate knowledge of diplomacy and protocol and royal ceremony and all those things Arden was totally lacking.

'Okay.' She knotted her fingers in her lap. 'What else?'

'Since you raise it, no lovers. Not even in secret. Once you marry me I expect complete loyalty.' His face had that stark look again, nostrils flared and jaw taut.

Arden stared. What difference could that make when this wasn't a real marriage? Then she realised she was about to protest just for the sake of it. She'd had no interest in men since Shakil/Idris, especially since Dawud's birth and her almost constant state of exhaustion. As for the frisson of erotic energy she felt when she was with Idris, she knew it was only a hangover from the past. She couldn't imagine herself ever having the time or inclination to fancy herself in love with anyone else.

'Okay.'

His eyebrows slanted up as if he'd expected an argument. 'And I'd rather you kept contact with my cousin to a minimum. Friendships between men and women aren't the norm in Zahrat and your friendship would be misinterpreted.'

'You don't ask much, do you?'

Idris said nothing, just waited for her response.

Once more she felt like refusing him, because surely what he asked was unreasonable. Except she'd already just said goodbye to one of her closest friends. Hamid had told her it didn't feel right to maintain their friendship once she married his cousin. Reading between the lines Arden knew he was hurt she'd chosen Idris. Whichever way she looked at it, her friendship with Hamid was in the past.

'Very well,' she muttered, 'I'll avoid contact with Hamid.' She paused, waiting for more. Except suddenly she couldn't take any more. Arden shot to her feet. 'If that's all, I'd like to be alone now. I'm tired from the trip.'

She was already heading for the door when his words pulled her up short.

'That's not quite all.'

'Yes?' She tried to guess what other condition he'd put on their arrangement. Limiting contact with her other friends perhaps? Or her freedom of movement? Wearily Arden pushed her shoulders back and turned, ready to fight for her rights.

'The wedding.'

'Yes?' *The wedding.* Not *our* wedding. The formal ceremony that would seal her fate and Dawud's. A tremor shot from her nape to the soles of her feet.

'It will be held in ten days.' His tone was even

and unemotional. Everything Arden didn't feel at
the prospect of marriage.

'So soon?' She pressed a palm to her chest
where her heart nosedived.

He shrugged. 'There's no point waiting. The
sooner this situation is settled the better.'

Situation being code for *scandal*. For an unwanted wife and an illegitimate son.

'Don't worry, all the arrangements will be taken
care of.'

In other words she'd have no say in her own
wedding.

Arden told herself that suited her perfectly. 'And
if I want to invite anyone?'

'Let Ashar know and he'll organise the invita-
tions.'

'I will.' She paused. 'That's all now?'

A tiny frown settled on Idris's brow. Why? Had
he expected her to make demands about the size
of the cake or the colour scheme? As far as Arden
was concerned it was far better someone else organised the nuptial extravaganza. She didn't have
the stomach for it.

'No, that's all.'

'Good. Then I'll see you later.'

She needn't have worried about Idris coming to
her room. For ten days she never saw him alone.

So much for the rogue idea he might want her
in his bed.

At least he was serious about building a relationship with his son. He'd breakfast with them then stop by after Dawud's bath to play a game or read a story in his own language. The gleam in Idris's eyes when he was with Dawud, the rich, enveloping sound of his laughter, tugged her back to those halcyon days on Santorini. Except, unlike *their* affair, this would last. For, to her surprise, she saw something like love in Idris's expression when he looked at their son, not duty. Their connection was real and growing. It brought a lump to her throat, seeing them together. She'd done the right thing—Dawud needed his dad too.

Inevitably though, Ashar waited in the wings, reminding Idris of his next meeting, making her wonder when he ever stopped.

Arden told herself she was grateful. She didn't *want* to see Idris alone. She had enough to do.

There were the language classes, classes on Zahrati customs and history, plus an increasing number of appointments and requests. Would she wear a gift of exquisite ivory silk from the silk weavers' guild at her wedding? Would she permit a women's embroidery group the honour of decorating the cloth with traditional bridal designs? Would she visit the school Leila, the girl she'd met during the procession, attended?

Her days were crammed and she lived on tenterhooks, knowing and hating the fact she'd inevitably make mistakes. It seemed impossible she'd ever succeed in this new role Idris expected of her. But if she failed would Dawud be accepted? That worry kept her trying, despite her reservations. Despite her exhaustion, she was too wired to sleep. Instead, each night she'd watch the shadows wheel across the vaulted ceiling above her bed.

Tonight, though, she'd sleep. Wedding preparations had begun at dawn and there would be not one but two ceremonies, one English and one Zahrati, followed by feasting and celebrations.

Butterflies, or perhaps a huge Zahrati eagle, emblem of the royal house, swooped and swirled in Arden's stomach as her attendants led her through the palace. As they approached the state rooms the exquisite furnishings became even more lavish, the scale of the interior growing till the cluster of twenty women were dwarfed.

With each step Arden felt the swish of fine fabric around her legs, the weight of heavy antique pearl necklaces so fabulous she hadn't believed they could be real. That was until her golden wedding coronet was placed on her head. Delicately made, it had flowers of ruby and sapphire, each with lustrous pearl petals.

Arden's neck was tight, her shoulders stiff and achy. She told herself it was fear that if she bent her head the coronet would slip off, despite the pins securing it.

But deep down she knew it was the thought of

marriage to Idris knotting tension within her. Her heart raced as she halted before vast gilded doors.

Was she doing the right thing?

She was doing the only thing that seemed right for her son.

Still she was more nervous even than when she'd gone into labour.

Her retinue fussed and fiddled, tweaking her long skirts, adjusting her necklaces and bracelets. One elegant lady took Arden's hand in both of hers and said something earnestly in a lilting voice. The other women murmured the same words, smiling, and she guessed it was a blessing.

She was about to ask what they'd said when the doors swung open and sound assaulted her. Laughter, music, voices. Her eyes widened. She'd seen the Hall of a Thousand Pillars before. It was one of the most spectacular rooms in the palace, but never had she seen it filled to capacity. It looked and sounded as if the whole city had crowded in.

Arden stood, dazed. She swallowed hard and told herself she would not flee.

Abruptly all sound ceased as if someone had switched off a soundtrack. Every head turned towards her. She breathed deep, telling herself to enter, but her feet stuck to the floor.

She heard a noise—the steady pace of the man approaching her, tall and magnificent in traditional robes, dazzling in white and gold.

Arden's heart stuttered as he filled her vision, so imposing, so attractive. She reminded herself this was a sham marriage, perpetrated to protect their son. But as Idris smiled and took her hand, heat poured through her. Her pulse leapt and she leaned towards him, as naturally as years ago when she'd loved him with all her youthful heart.

'You are beautiful, Arden. Breathtaking.' The words were for her alone as his lips brushed her temple.

That was when she realised how dangerous this was. How easy it would be to believe the fantasy that she and Idris shared something more than the need to protect their boy.

It was as if she *wanted* to believe Idris desired her, respected her, loved her.

Arden closed her eyes, summoning the courage she'd built over the years when she needed to face down the odds and be strong for Dawud.

When she opened them Idris was still there, still looking like the answer to every woman's prayer.

But he was her partner in a contract, not her lover. Together they would protect Dawud and give him the future he deserved.

'Thank you for the compliment.' It was only encouragement to see her through a difficult day. 'And you look spectacular too.' She let him lead her into the vast room, head up, spine straight and a smile fixed on her lips.

* * *

Arden swayed with tiredness as her attendants stripped the exquisite ivory and gold wedding gown away and led her to the bathroom. Steam curled invitingly from the bath in the centre of the room and blush-pink rose petals covered the surface of the water.

A bath fit for a royal bride.

Suddenly all the pomp, glamour and luxury of the day mocked her.

She needed to be alone.

She'd done her best to play her part, smiling through the endless speeches and ceremonies. Not flinching when Idris took her hand and led her to a fabulous gilded throne. Nor when he fed her delicacies from his plate, his eyes shining with a look anyone who didn't know the truth would interpret as desire. Only Arden knew it was satisfaction that they'd got through the day without a hitch.

But enough was enough.

'Thanks very much, but no.' She shook her head as a servant approached, ready to attend her in the bath. 'I prefer to bathe alone.'

Still it took a few moments to convince them she was serious. When they'd gone she stripped off her lace underwear, pinned her hair and sank into the bath.

A sigh escaped. Or was it a groan? The warm water did marvellous things to muscles twisted

with tension. For the first time in hours she began
to relax in the bliss of the fragrant bath.

She was dozing, her head lolling against the
cushioned headrest when she heard the door open.

'I'm fine,' she murmured drowsily. 'I don't need
any help.'

'Not even to scrub your back?' The voice, deep
and soft like a ribbon of plush velvet, stroked her
bare skin.

CHAPTER EIGHT

WATER SPLASHED AS she sat up, twisting towards the door.

'Idris!' It was the barest wisp of sound. Her voice disintegrated as she took him in.

Gone were the white robes he'd worn for their wedding. Now there were only loose trousers of fine cotton, slung low across his hips. His torso was bare, a muscled, glorious expanse of dark gold with a smattering of ebony hair across his pectorals, resolving into a thin, dark line bisecting his abdomen. Arden remembered being fascinated by that line, and where it led, in the week they'd once spent together.

She swallowed hard.

As she watched, muscles rippled across his chest and abdomen, as if stirred by her stare.

Instantly she dragged her gaze up. It collided with a bright, intense look that reminded her she was naked.

Arden drew her knees up to her breasts, looping an arm tight around her legs.

'What are you doing here?'

His mouth curled in a smile that drove a sexy groove down one cheek and made her aware of a sudden ache of emptiness high between her legs.

It was the first genuine smile he'd given her in four years and it made her feel like the lovestruck innocent she'd been on Santorini, all breathless anticipation and hammering heart.

She hated that he had such power over her.

'Why are you here, Idris?' Her voice was sharp.

'I thought that was obvious.' He walked closer and crouched down so his breath feathered her face. 'I'm here to help my wife bathe.'

'Wife in name only. And I'm perfectly able to take a bath alone.'

'But why should you when you have a husband willing and able to assist?'

'Husband in name only.' Arden gritted her teeth, annoyed at the way her body reacted to the rich, clean scent of sandalwood and man. As if four years hadn't passed. As if she were still besotted with him.

'On the contrary, our marriage is as real as two wedding ceremonies can make it.'

She shook her head, not in the mood for semantics. 'You agreed not to come into my room without permission.' It was a struggle to keep her voice even. All those years he'd visited her in her dreams, taunting her with the knowledge that, despite being an exhausted single mum, she was also a woman with needs. Now here he was in the too tempting flesh.

He braced his forearm on the edge of the bath, inches from her bare shoulder, and she shivered as if he'd touched her. 'Ah. That's where you're wrong. You mentioned that, but if you think back you'll remember it was one condition I never agreed to.'

He lifted his other hand and trailed the tips of his fingers in the water near her knees. He didn't touch her but the ripples he made were like tiny caresses teasing her flesh.

'Stop that!' He stilled and Arden dragged in a shuddery breath. 'Stop playing word games. You're not welcome here and you know it.'

Yet as she spoke Arden felt excitement rip through her at his heavy-lidded look. It stirred her body to tingling anticipation for his touch and, despite everything, for the unique sense of belonging and well-being she'd known in his arms. She reminded herself that was illusory but still her body trembled, igniting anger.

'We married for pragmatic reasons. Don't try to pretend this is about love.' She wasn't foolish enough to fall for that.

Idris shook his head, his expression too close to smug for her liking. 'That doesn't mean we need to keep our distance. Why should we when we want each other?'

'I don't—' Her voice cut out when his hand

swirled through the water to caress her knee. Instantly a powerful judder of response racked her.

From a touch to her knee! That should be impossible. But so too should the avid look on Idris's face, as if he wanted to lean in and gobble her up, or maybe taste her slowly. Another quiver coursed through her and she pulled sideways, away from his touch, wrapping her arms tighter round her folded legs.

'Why don't you amuse yourself with one of your lovers and leave me alone?'

'One of my...?' For the first time Idris seemed lost for words.

'I don't want you in my suite.' Even though her body cried out for him. It was a shocking realisation but she'd get over it, just as she'd got over so much in the past.

'First—' he leaned in, all trace of a smile gone '—this is *our* suite. My bathroom and dressing room are on the other side of the bedroom.' Behind what she'd thought were blank walls? 'Rather than have you and Dawud settle into guest rooms then move after the wedding, I thought it would be less disruptive for Dawud in particular not to have to move twice. I've been sleeping elsewhere till the wedding.'

Dimly, part of her applauded his concern for their son. But mainly she was stunned by the revelation he'd expected her to share his bed all this time.

'Second, I don't have lovers waiting in the wings. I haven't had a lover in...' he shook his head '...a long time. I've been busy with other things.' He drew in a deep breath that expanded his chest mightily, reminding her of his sheer physical strength and beauty.

'Do you really think I'd go to another woman on my wedding night?' He looked angry, as if she'd insulted him.

'Why not? Unless you think because I'm conveniently close I'm available. If so, you're completely wrong.' Old bitterness welled. She understood now that Idris hadn't deliberately avoided her all those years ago but it was hard to erase the pain of rejection. 'You can't ignore me for weeks then swan in here, expecting intimacy.'

'Ignore you! I've seen you every day.' His face drew tight in that dangerous expression she'd privately dubbed his bronzed warrior look. 'I've spent every waking hour trying to smooth the way so that our marriage is viewed positively instead of as a hole-and-corner affair. So you and Dawud are accepted and welcomed. So we can live in peace and safety if I manage to salvage this treaty.'

Idris looked proud and forbidding. Yet Arden's heart leapt. There was something incredibly invigorating about being at the epicentre of all that furious energy.

But it wasn't enough.

'I'm not some *duty*.' She tipped back her head

and glared. 'I'm a *person*. You can't treat me like a stranger then expect me to have sex with you.'

The harsh words jarred. Once she'd thought of it as making love. Glorious, heaven-touching love. But she'd learned a lot since those days of innocence. Idris had never loved her, though she'd been besotted enough to throw in her job and follow him to Paris.

His nostrils flared as he bent closer.

There was something incredibly intimate about the fact he was inhaling the scent of her skin and the exotic cinnamon and pomegranate wash they'd used on her hair this morning. He was drawing her in and, despite her anger, her body was eager for him to devour her.

'You think I treated you as a stranger?' His voice dropped to a deep note that wove its way into every sense receptor in her body. 'You think I ignored you?'

Idris tilted his head from side to side in a slow, emphatic negative. His hand closed around her knee in a deliberate, possessive hold that stilled her breath.

She'd never been attuned to any man as she was to Idris. Even wanting to break free, she couldn't deny the connection between them.

'For ten days I've worked myself into a stupor rather than come to your bed.' His voice grated, harsh and low. 'For ten days I've done the right thing, honouring you as a bride should be honoured.

For ten days I've tortured myself with the sight and sound and scent of you.' He paused, inhaling again, and another of those erotic quivers coursed through her. 'But I didn't touch because I respected you. And I wanted everyone to know that.'

Idris leaned in, so close his dark eyes and golden skin filled her vision.

Arden was drowning in a sea of sensation. His touch on her bare skin, the intoxicating promise of sensual pleasure in his velvety eyes, the scent of him, potent male with a hint of sandalwood, even the sound of his breathing, steady and strong, dragged her down into a well of desire.

'And because you want me I'm supposed to welcome you with open arms?' Fear spiked. She suspected surrendering herself physically to Idris would be more complete, more irrevocable even than marrying him. A piece of paper, however important, was nothing compared with the intimacy of sharing herself.

'No, *habibti*. You'll welcome me because you want me too. That hasn't changed, has it? The desire is as strong as ever.'

Arden opened her mouth to deny it when she realised he'd taken his hand from her knee. She felt it now underwater. Deep underwater.

Unerringly his big hand stroked between her legs, insinuating itself between her thighs and finding the spot where the heavy, sensual pulse of arousal struck hard and fast at the core of her.

Arden gasped and stiffened, clamping her thighs tight. It was too late. He was already there, stroking that most secret place with a sure yet delicate touch that sent whorls of excitement spiralling through her.

'Stop that!' She made a grab for his forearm underwater but couldn't shift him. Instead she felt the fine movement of tendons as his fingers flexed and stroked.

The sensation was too unsettling, as if she contributed to her own weakness, and she ripped her hand away, clutching the side of the tub instead, gasping.

She made herself stare up into his gleaming eyes. 'I don't want this.' But it wasn't true. Torn pride demanded she reject him. But the lonely, needy woman who'd once found magic with this man stirred to life.

'If I believed that for a second I'd walk out the door.' Abruptly the stroking fingers stopped, ending the addictive pressure on that sensitive nub, and to her dismay Arden realised her hips were tilting, lifting up towards his touch, pressing herself against him.

The tiny movement was utterly telling.

She stifled a sob of distress, of shame laced with despair. *She wanted him again...still.* As if those four lonely years had never been.

Yet instead of gloating over it, Idris said gently,

'Let me do this for you. You've been wound so tight all day I thought you'd break.'

Arden prised open tight lips, though what she'd have said she never discovered because he touched her again. This time he delved while his thumb circled, and sensation shot through her, making her jump and her breath snatch.

Instinctively she grabbed for support, one hand on the rim of the bath, the other on a hot, bony shoulder, padded with muscle.

'That's it,' he whispered, his voice at the same time soothing and incredibly sensual. 'Hold on tight.'

Eyes like the midnight sky held hers. This close she saw soft dark brown against black pupils. If it weren't for the fierce intensity of that stare she'd call it tender. Tender enough to soothe her lacerated, confused soul.

Then there was no time for thought as, with one deft stroke, Idris toppled her over the edge. Delight exploded, razing her defences and her self protecting lies.

Dark eyes held hers as she rode wave after wave of pleasure till, at the end, she had no place left to hide. And no energy to maintain the fiction that she didn't want him every bit as much as she had four years ago.

Triumph warred with tenderness as Arden came apart at his touch. He felt each juddering spasm heard each snatched gasp, her sweet breath was warm on his face, her hand clawing at his shoulder so hard she probably scored his flesh. And through it all those remarkable aquamarine eyes locked with his, drawing him into ecstasy till he feared he might explode, just watching her come.

It felt as if he'd waited a lifetime to possess her, not a mere couple of weeks. It was a miracle he hadn't simply stripped off and taken her where she lay in the water.

Except, even now on their wedding day, Arden didn't make anything easy. Accusing him of having a lover tonight of all nights! What sort of man did she think he was?

It infuriated him and slashed at his pride that she'd believe such a thing. He'd done nothing but treat her with courtesy and respect and still she...

She blinked and to his amazement moisture welled, drowning her lovely eyes. The sight jabbed something sharp and hard through his gut, skewering him. Her mouth twisted as if in anguish and she swung her head away so all he saw were damp wisps of rose gold hair clinging to her pinkened shoulder and throat.

She regretted this?

Idris slowly drew his hand back, feeling a final, needy clench of her muscles. Despite the bliss he'd given her, he hadn't broken down Arden's resistance. He knew he'd hurt her terribly, that she'd suffered because of his unintentional desertion.

But he'd been sure she was ready to start afres
Sure she wanted him as he craved her.

Had he really expected this to be so easy?

Somewhere Fate laughed at him and his foo
ish ego.

He looked at her ripe mouth, caught at one co
ner by white teeth as if even now she fought t
bliss he'd bestowed. Her body might be ready f
him, but emotionally Arden wasn't.

Memory slammed into him, of her bent hea
and defeated voice as she spoke to his cous
on the phone. She'd said he wasn't her lover, b
clearly there was something between them, or ha
been, till Idris entered her life again.

He got to his feet, towering above her. In t
sunken bath her milky pale body, flushed he
and there with the rose blush of sexual satiatio
was too much like the erotic fantasies he endure
night after night.

Breathing quickly, trying to ignore the fragran
of sweet woman, he pivoted away, wrenching h
mind from the need to possess her.

'Idris?' Her voice, husky and soft, tantalise
'Where are you going?'

His shoulders set like granite.

'I won't force myself on an unwilling woman
The knowledge she didn't want him scalded h
pride and something else, something unnamed th
hurt far more than he'd believed possible.

Idris heard the rush of sluicing water and fe

warm drops splash the backs of his legs, sticking thin cotton trousers to steamy hot skin.

'*Unwilling* would be an exaggeration.' She was breathless. 'I was so sure I didn't want this. Now I don't know what to think.' The pain in her voice tore at him.

He closed his eyes, seeking strength. His groin was rock-hard, throbbing with the need, not just for release, but for *Arden*. He wanted to be inside her, feeling her come again, grabbing him tight with the undulating waves of her next climax. He wanted her complete surrender. He wanted her screaming his name—*his* name and no one else's.

He didn't think he had the stamina for any more celibate nights with her under his roof.

Hands clenched, he spun round.

Everything, his thoughts, his determination, even his pride, melted. Only his body grew impossibly harder at the sight of her, standing up to her thighs in water. Her hair glowed, framing her flushed face. Her beautiful Cupid's bow lips parted as if eager to taste him. Her eyes shone brighter than any gems in the royal treasury and her body was a symphony of delicate femininity. Between her thighs was that V of rose gold, hiding the gate to Paradise.

His gaze swept back up, pausing, fascinated by the delicate, shimmery striations just visible on her belly—marks where her satin-soft skin had stretched to carry his child.

A bolt of lightning struck down, welding his feet to the floor.

He'd never seen a more desirable woman, never felt such primitive possessiveness.

'Don't toy with me, Arden.' His voice was strangled.

She took a slow breath that lifted her tip-tilted breasts towards him. 'I'm not.' She swallowed and he watched the convulsive movement of her throat. 'I thought I could keep my distance. Keep separate. But I can't.' Her mouth crumpled at the edges and his chest squeezed. 'I was wrong. I want you, *still*.'

She didn't sound happy about it. He recognised the same conflicting emotions he felt—tension, need and something akin to fear at the force of what was between them. From the first he'd felt *more* with Arden. Every need, every emotion had been more intense, more real.

Arden held out her arms, slick and shining with water. 'Take me.' Her eyes held his and power jolted through him.

He needed no second urging. In one swift movement he scooped her up, one arm at her back and the other beneath her knees. Her wet, glorious body against his was a form of perfect torture as he marched across the marble floor and into the next room.

The cover of the vast bed had been pulled back, the sheets scattered with delicate petals.

There was nothing delicate about Idris's movements. Four huge strides took him to the bed. An instant later Arden landed on the mattress, her breath expelling in a soft *oof* of air as he followed her down, pressing against her slick body, revelling in the slide of smooth flesh against his.

A groan sounded in his ears. His? Hers? It didn't matter, for now she was touching him, her hands skidding over his shoulders and down his back, so low they slipped beneath thin cotton to cup his buttocks.

Instinctively he thrust forward, hard and high, revelling in the slide of flesh against flesh, heat against silken coolness. Her fingers curled tight, grabbing, as her thighs lifted, cradling around him in a damp caress.

Idris had a momentary impression of sultry, half-lidded eyes, the eyes of a temptress inviting a lover, then Arden's hands slipped up his back, cupping the back of his neck to pull his head down.

Their lips fused and this time it was Arden setting the pace, Arden angling her mouth against his, a delectable hum of need vibrating from her throat and filling his mouth. Her tongue seduced his, eager and sensual, and he felt the power of that erotic connection right through him. His erection pressed heavily against her belly, his hips shifting with the unbearable tension.

Dimly Idris registered his complete loss of command over his body. It was moving of its own volition, incited by this sensual woman to abandon any hope of control or expertise. Instinct and hunger drove him. Already he was fumbling at the drawstring of his trousers, shoving the material down, scrabbling to be free.

He was just lowering himself back to Arden's delicious body when ingrained habit halted him.

'What's wrong?' Her words were the faintest, muffled sound in his mouth.

'Condom.' He paused, dragging air into tight lungs. Even as he said it he knew he wanted nothing more than to be inside her, no barriers between them. The thought was so arousing he scowled, drawing on every ounce of control not to shatter prematurely.

Idris wrenched away, lunging for the bedside table. Since they hadn't had that vital conversation about future pregnancies, he'd taken the precaution of bringing a box of protection. A large box.

'You were so sure of me?' Her voice held an edge.

Idris rolled on the condom, gritting his teeth at his sensitivity, then turned to her. Deliberately he slid his knee over hers, dragging it towards him, opening her thighs. His palm settled on her soft belly.

'Sure of *us*.' His voice was gruff. Speaking grew harder each second. 'This is mutual, Arden. You must know that. I've been burning for you since I saw you again in London.'

Veiled eyes held his, as if she sifted the truth of

his words. Then he lifted his hand to capture her breast and her breath hissed in.

She was so soft, so delicate, so perfectly made for him. How could he have gone all these years without finding her again and inviting her into his bed?

Idris lowered his head to capture her nipple between his teeth, grazing it gently, and she almost catapulted from the bed. He leaned over her, covering her, enjoying the slide of his body against her slick flesh.

This time he flicked her nipple with his tongue, cupping her satiny breast, overwhelmed by the familiarity of her. Beneath the fruit and flower aromas of Zahrat from the bath, it was the scent of Arden that befuddled his brain. The feel of her—familiar as if they'd shared a bed just days, not years, before, the tiny growl of arousal at the back of her throat that made his erection pulse eagerly against her thigh.

His hand tightened around her breast, his teeth nipped harder. Delicacy was beyond him. What he felt was too primal, too urgent to be contained.

Yet she welcomed him, grabbing his shoulders and urging him higher. He caught a flash of aquamarine between slitted eyelids, felt her restless bucking, heard those urgent mews of pleasure and knew she couldn't wait either.

Idris shifted to lie within her cradling hips, the bulk of his weight on his arms. His eyes rolled closed when she tilted her pelvis, grinding herself against him.

Then there was nothing but instinct and pleasure, pure pleasure, as he nudged her entrance and thrust home with one sure stroke.

She cried out, a husky sound of welcome that he tasted as he took her lips, possessing her mouth in mimicry of the way he took her body.

Arden wrapped her arms behind his back, pulling him in. He slid further still when she lifted her legs and locked them around his buttocks.

The feel of her surrounding him everywhere was too much. He withdrew a fraction then surged high and hard and the ripples of pleasure began.

Fire caught his throat and chest, flames flickered in his blood at the tightness, the slick heat, the absolute perfection of her taking him in.

Another thrust and the ripples became shudders racking them both, making them jerk and shake together, turning fire into an explosion of white-hot ecstasy. Idris swallowed her shout of elation as he pulsed within her then disintegrated into tiny splinters of being. His world shattered in the exquisite pleasure-pain of sensation stronger than anything he could remember.

CHAPTER NINE

ARDEN WAS OUT for the count, limp with satiation, yet Idris couldn't keep his hands off her. She'd slept at least an hour and he was only human. He'd already fumbled on the bedside table for another condom and sheathed himself, yet still she hadn't stirred.

Idris ran his palm over the sinuous curve from her shoulder down her ribcage to her narrow waist then up to her hip. Lying on her side, that intoxicating female outline was even more pronounced.

His hand drifted from her hip to her belly, feathering the soft down between her legs, and she sighed in her sleep, shifting and stretching. He smiled, closing the gap between them. Immediately he felt her buttocks press back, cushioning his erection.

His breath stalled. His heart pounded so hard she must feel it hammering against her back.

'Shakil?' Her voice was a drowsy mumble that made him smile, though he registered chagrin that she'd used his boyish nickname.

Even half-awake she knew it was him. He'd hated the thought of the other men who'd no doubt been in her life. It was unreasonable, but he wanted to be the only man she'd ever had.

He remembered his soaring elation, the unexpected humility of learning he was her first lover. That had to explain this deeply proprietorial response he hadn't been able to conquer since London.

That and the fact she's your wife.

Your life has changed for ever.

Yet the dread voice of reason couldn't dim the sheer excitement of having her in his bed.

His.

Idris slid his fingers down, following that downy arrow to her sensitive nub. Her breath caught on a sigh and her pelvis tilted into his touch. She might be barely awake but she wanted him. He pressed his mouth to her neck, tasting the rich sweetness that was hers alone. Then her earlobe, scraping it gently with his teeth, and she shivered delicately, her back bowing again, arching that lush bottom into his groin.

But it wasn't enough. 'Tell me what you want.' He needed to hear it again.

'You. I want you.' Her voice was husky with desire and it aroused him as much as her sexy body. More. Her admission was potently exciting, even though he'd observed, as long ago as London, the attraction she tried to deny.

She wriggled, pressing herself against his groin, creating a firestorm of wanting.

In one swift movement he rose to his knees, grabbing her hips and lifting her so she knelt on the bed before him, his hands planted hard on her hips, caging her to him. Idris waited, breath bated, partly to give himself time to regain some control and partly to see Arden's reaction.

She bunched the sheet in her outstretched hands and shimmied her hips back and up into his pelvis.

Idris swallowed a groan of pain. It was exquisite torture, bliss and unbearable longing, kneeling here, with her so inviting before him. Impossible not to look down, to see her peach of a backside pushing at his erection.

Once again the firestorm hit—a blast of longing, of desperate arousal stronger than anything he could recall.

Had it always been like this? He'd thought his memories of their affair were coloured by the crises that followed, turning it into a glorious, perfect interlude because of the grimness immediately afterwards. He'd thought he'd imagined the perfection of their passion and that sense of being in the one place in the world he needed to be. But as he guided himself inside her, one hand welded to her hip, his rapt gaze on the erotic sight of their joining, he knew memory hadn't exaggerated.

Arden gave another shimmy of her hips so he lodged deeper in her welcoming warmth, and Idris knew once more the panicked delight of impending climax.

Where was his patience? His sensual prowess? His ability to savour sex and please his partner?

Gone the second Arden welcomed him into her body.

Desperately he bowed over her, one hand seeking her pouting breast, cupping it and rolling her nipple between thumb and forefinger so she jerked against him, her breath a hiss of air. His other hand arrowed down between her thighs, straight to her moist centre, pressing down on that sensitive nub as he withdrew then hammered home again, right to her core.

Her hands on the sheets were white-knuckled, her movements as she pushed back rough and urgent. He clamped his hand harder around her breast and she gasped, rolling her head back. Instantly he was there, leaning in, biting her earlobe, in time with the thrust of his body and the hard circling of his fingers.

'Yes!' Her triumphant shout filled the night. 'Yes, yes, yes. Shakil!' She grabbed his hand on her breast, pressing it to her as her body began to quiver around him. The quivers became shudders, caressing him, milking him with a sweet ferocity he couldn't resist.

With a groan of rapture he grabbed her hips and spilled himself, hard and fast into her slickness.

His last thought before he collapsed on her and

rolled them both onto their sides, still joined, was that next time, surely, he'd be able to take it slow.

Arden squinted against the light. Surely it wasn't time to get up. Had they managed to sleep at all?

Heat bit her skin from her scalp to her toes and everywhere in between as she remembered the urgency with which they'd made love. With such desperation it made her think of stories she'd heard about people who'd survived some terrible life or death event and were driven by instinct to procreate.

Once she'd believed love was the reason she and Shakil had made the earth tremble on its axis. Now she realised sex and love needn't intersect. There was something about the man she'd married, something she responded to every time, that made the sex earth-shatteringly wonderful.

Sex, she reminded herself. Not lovemaking.

Disappointment eddied. With herself for not completely banishing that old yearning for love. A touch was all it had taken for Idris to smash through her caution. She'd acted as if the last four years had never been!

She opened her eyes wider, taking in the rumpled bed, the sun streaming in the arched windows and the complete absence of her husband.

There might have been rose petals strewn on the bed but this wasn't a hearts and flowers marriage.

It was a cold-hearted convenience for the sake of their son and her husband's reputation.

'You look pensive this morning.'

Idris strode towards the bed, damp hair slicked back, buttoning his shirt.

Instantly Arden's heart fluttered and her stomach gave that little quiver of anticipation she despised. No matter how often she told herself she felt nothing for Idris, her body betrayed her.

She needed to conquer or at least control her response. If she didn't she feared it would make her completely vulnerable.

'I need more sleep.'

Except one glance at him and it wasn't sleep on her mind. A pulse twitched between her legs and she shifted beneath the sheets, drawing his gaze. When his eyes met hers they gleamed hot and hungry and Arden found herself wondering at his stamina. How he found the energy even to walk she didn't know.

'Then sleep. I need to farewell those guests who stayed overnight.'

Reluctantly Arden dragged herself up against the pillows, drawing the cotton sheet around her, ignoring his raised eyebrow that reminded her he was intimately acquainted with every bare inch of her.

'If you wait fifteen minutes I'll come too.' Arden felt imprisoned in this new world that had been foisted on her, and by last night's proof of weakness. She didn't want to stay here, brooding, with the bedroom walls closing in. Besides, she had to start as she meant to go on. For Dawud's sake she'd fulfil her new royal role, as far as she could.

'No need.' His mouth widened into a smile that could only be described as smug. 'No one expects to see you today.'

Arden frowned. 'Yet they expect to see you?'

He grabbed his watch from the small table covered in condom wrappers, smiling at her as he strapped it on. The sight was ordinary yet intimate, reminding her they really were tied in marriage, husband and wife, come what may.

'As a vigorous man in the prime of life I'm supposed to take a wedding night in my stride.' His eyes flickered and Arden wondered what he was thinking.

'And the bride isn't?'

He shrugged and there was no mistaking the satisfaction in his tone. 'A new bride might be a little…tender, and need rest.'

'After a *vigorous* night with her new husband?' By a miracle Arden didn't blush. She was more than a little tender. She felt exhausted but also dangerously exhilarated, which disturbed even more.

'Precisely.' His high wattage smile rocked her back against the pillows. 'There'd be dismay if you appeared. People would think I hadn't done my husbandly duty.'

His words pummelled her. It had been husbandly

duty, nothing more. Except, she guessed, surveying his lazy satisfaction, pride and the masculine ability to take pleasure wherever it was offered.

And she'd offered. She'd been as eager for Idris as he was for her. The difference was that to him she was just an available body. For her there still lingered shreds of the sentiment she'd once felt for him.

She had to change that fast, before she fell for that old romantic daydream.

'You never told me about that day in Santorini. What message you passed on.' The words blurted out before she realised she'd formed them. Suddenly it was vital she knew the whole truth.

'Sorry?' Idris was halfway to the door but turned at her words. 'What message?'

'You said you'd arranged for someone to meet me four years ago. At the rendezvous that last day when you couldn't meet me.'

'That's right.' Slowly he nodded.

'But you never told me what you'd instructed him to say.'

Dark eyes bored into hers. 'It hardly matters now. What matters is our future.'

Oh, it matters. From his sudden stillness, she guessed it mattered very much.

'Humour me. Was he going to take me to meet you in Paris or…?'

Idris breathed deep, his chest expanding as he took his time answering.

'I didn't go to Paris. My uncle was dangerously ill so I returned here.' He swung towards the door. But Arden wasn't letting him off. She'd spent years wondering about that day.

'So what was your message for me?'

He paused. For the first time Arden felt Idris was at a loss. Yet this was the man who took international scandals in his stride, even the discovery of a son and a forced wedding.

His gaze settled at a point beyond her head. 'To give my regrets and say we couldn't be together after all.'

Arden told herself she wasn't surprised, despite the chill clinging to her bones. 'To say goodbye.'

He nodded, his eyes briefly meeting hers. Then he exited the room.

It was what she'd expected—that, despite her girlish dreams, he'd planned to reject her that day. She, in her innocence, had fallen in love with the handsome stranger who'd swept her off her feet. But to him she'd been a mere holiday amusement. There'd never been any question of him taking her to his home. Her grand romance had been a fantasy.

Arden watched him leave and told herself she was grateful she'd finally unearthed the truth. What better time than now when, in the afterglow of Idris's lovemaking, she was in danger of reading too much into their intimacy?

He'd never wanted her as she'd wanted him. Never needed her.

Something inside her chest crumpled but she breathed through the pain.

It reinforced the lessons life had taught her. Those she cared about always ended up leaving her to fend for herself. First her parents. Then the foster parents who'd changed their mind about adopting her when they discovered they were expecting a child of their own.

Then Shakil.

Just as well she wasn't in love with him any more. She'd moved on, even if Idris could still make her feel more than she should.

The only person she loved, who loved her back, was her son. That, she reminded herself as she shoved the sheet aside and headed for the bathroom, was all she needed.

At least Idris was honest about his feelings, or lack of them. She was grateful for that. He made it clear their marriage was solely to scotch scandal and provide a solid future for Dawud.

In the bathroom she wrenched on the taps in the shower, spurning the idea of a languorous soak in the tub. The decadence of that sunken tub, and what had happened there last night, was too dangerous. She needed to ground herself. A shower, fresh clothes and time with Dawud. Then she'd apply herself to the long, daunting process of learning what was expected of a royal sheikha.

It didn't matter that she felt doomed to fail and completely overwhelmed. She bit back a silent scream of hurt and helplessness, refusing to let tears well. She had to find strength. She *had* to make this work. Dawud's future depended on it.

Idris found her, not in bed but playing with their son in a private courtyard.

He forced down disappointment. He'd returned as soon as he could, the image of her waiting for him in bed, her hair a golden cloud around bare milk-white breasts, had distracted him through the protracted farewells, leaving him aroused and edgy. Never had the tedium of official duties weighed so heavily. He'd all but thrust the last guests through the palace portals.

He squashed annoyance that she hadn't waited for him, naked. He should be grateful she was a caring mother. Right? Wasn't that what this marriage was all about?

But as he stepped from the shadows of the portico it wasn't their necessary marriage consuming his thoughts. It was sex, hot and urgent, with the woman who diverted him from all thoughts of duty.

'Baba!' He heard the cry as Dawud's beaming smile caught him full-on. There was a curious thud in the region of his chest, as if his heart had missed a beat then pounded out of rhythm. Then he was crouching, arms open, as his son hurried over, his dark hair tousled into the beginnings of curls—just like Idris's own hair if he let it grow.

'Watch out, he's wet!'

But Idris didn't mind. He closed his son in his embrace, ignoring the way the little wet body saturated his clothes.

His son.

Idris had been surprised from the first at the feelings the boy evoked. They grew every day. And they made everything, the hassle of organising a royal wedding in record time, the frowning disapproval of the old guard, even the strained relations with Ghizlan's father, fade to nothing. He was more determined than ever to secure peace, now it meant protecting his son.

'Baba.' Dawud lifted a hand to Idris's face, tiny fingers patting at his cheek and nose.

Idris laughed and caught Arden's surprise. It made him realise how rarely he laughed. Until Arden and Dawud arrived he'd spent all his time working. Yet he'd enjoyed the last weeks with them, despite the enormous strain of dealing with crises.

He greeted Dawud in Arabic and was amazed when Dawud answered in kind, lisping a little on the unfamiliar words.

'He remembered what I taught him!'

'He's a quick learner.'

Idris nodded, taken aback by the swell of pride at his boy's cleverness. Did all fathers feel this way? His father had never doted on him, caught up instead in his schemes for personal pleasure. Idris had been closer to his tutors, including the hard men who'd taught him the ancient arts of warfare.

'He likes to please you too.'

Arden's voice made him look up. She stood, hands clasped tight as if to stop from reaching out to grab their son. The twist of her lips told him it wasn't simple pride she felt. Didn't she trust him with Dawud?

Idris had worried he'd get this fathering thing wrong with no role model to guide him. So far he seemed to be doing okay but would instinct be enough as Dawud grew?

Yet even as the familiar doubt surfaced he noticed the way Arden's wet blouse had turned transparent, giving him a tantalising view of luscious breasts in a lacy half cup bra. She took his breath away every time.

Idris stood, lifting Dawud into his arms, but the boy wriggled to be let go. That was when Idris noticed the plastic toy boats floating in the shallow pools inlaid with tiny tiles of lapis lazuli, marble and gold.

His lips quirked as he put Dawud down and watched him plump with a splash into the couple of inches of water, immediately absorbed in his game with the boats.

'You don't mind him playing here?' Arden's expression was guarded. 'There's no playground but

I thought he couldn't hurt anything here, if he's supervised.'

Idris thought of the painstaking, delicate work that had gone into creating the ornamental pools with their exquisite sixteenth century mosaics. They were national treasures, one of the reasons for the palace's heritage status.

'I think it's a perfect place to play with toy boats. I wish I'd thought of it when I was young.' When he was a kid there was no way any of his royal uncle's entourage would dream of letting a small boy enjoy such freedoms. 'We must see about a proper playground. Perhaps with a sandpit and a climbing frame?'

He watched with pleasure as some of the tension bled from Arden's stiff frame. 'That would be perfect. Thank you.'

That confirmed what he'd known from the first—the way to Arden's good graces was through their son. Even after a night spent in Idris's arms, she'd looked anything but relaxed until he started talking about plans for Dawud.

Regret stabbed. Was that really their only connection? Their boy? It should please him that Dawud was so important to her, yet pride demanded she acknowledge his own place in her life.

Then he saw the tension in her twined hands. Of course she wanted him. He couldn't have asked for a more willing, generous lover. But they were strangers still. He needed to give her time to adjust to her new life.

Idris settled himself on the warm flagstones behind their son, reaching forward to propel a tiny sailboat forward. Dawud crowed with delight, splashing his appreciation and chattering. Idris joined in, enjoying the game, heedless of the water drenching his formal robes. Dawud's excitement, the laughter, the spray of water in the sunlight, created a sense of well-being, as if for once there weren't a million tasks clamouring for Idris's attention. As if this simple joy was all that mattered.

Arden dragged a chair into the shade of an ornamental tree and sat on the other side of the pool, watching. It struck Idris that, no matter what the law said about his rights as a father, she was working hard to allow him access to his son. Not every woman would make it so easy.

'It must be hard, sharing Dawud after all this time.'

Her eyes widened, their pale depths glittering in surprise. 'I...' She shrugged. 'It takes a little getting used to. In the past I was the only one he'd run to. Me and his nursery teacher.'

'Not Hamid?'

The question was a mistake. Arden tensed and the easy atmosphere fractured.

'Hamid was always kind to Dawud but he never got down on the ground to play with him.'

Her words pleased Idris. It was petty to compare

the relationship he'd begun to build with his son against his cousin's. Yet he couldn't fully excise that sliver of jealousy over the time Hamid had spent with Arden and Dawud in London.

'Hamid was a friend. He never acted like Dawud's father—'

'And he wasn't your lover?' Snaking distrust wound through him.

'I've said it before and won't say it again. You'll have to take my word for it.' Her chin lifted and her eyes flashed and Idris had never wanted her more.

Her stare might spit fire but, aware of their son playing between them, she kept her voice low. It struck him that his hunger for her wasn't purely physical. There was something about the way she protected Dawud that got to him at a level every bit as primal as sex.

The mother of his son. A woman who'd do anything for their boy, even marry a stranger in a strange land.

Pride throbbed through Idris. Pride and admiration. And, as ever, that undertow of desire.

'I apologise, Arden. I should have taken your word from the first.' Despite the remnants of jealousy, he believed her. What did she have to gain by lying? Even Hamid had made it clear they hadn't been lovers. Idris had to conquer this dog-in-the-manger jealousy. It was completely out of character.

Arden provoked emotions that were unique—both positive and negative. He wanted to understand why. Understand her.

'Why did you call him Dawud? A name from my country, not yours?' She'd believed he'd abandoned her, so it was odd she'd given their son a name that linked him to Idris's homeland.

She lifted her shoulders, her gaze veering away. 'I went to an exhibition of beautiful antique artefacts from Zahrat and discovered one of your rulers had been King Dawud. I liked the name and wanted our boy to have some connection to your country. To own a link to his father's heritage as well as mine.'

'That's very generous, given what you thought of me.' Idris frowned. 'It surprised me.' And it was one of the reasons he'd thought Hamid her lover.

'Wouldn't you have accepted him with an English name?'

Idris stared her down till her cheeks flushed pink. Surely she couldn't believe he'd ever deny his son? 'I would have accepted him no matter what. But it makes it easier for our people when he has a name they recognise.'

Again that little shrug. 'It's close enough to the English name David if he wanted to change it later. But I thought he'd appreciate some link to his father's culture.'

'That's why you began learning Arabic? To teach our boy?' Idris should have made the connection. Now it struck him how significant her actions had been. Even believing herself deserted, Arden had tried to build a bridge between their son and a cultural inheritance to which she was an outsider. Idris leaned closer, fascinated by such generosity of spirit.

'I wanted Dawud to feel he belonged, to feel a sense of connection, even if he never knew his father. I believe it's vital for a child.'

The way she spoke, the determined glint in her eyes, suggested this wasn't just about Dawud. Idris raked his memory for what he knew of Arden's history. All he knew was that she had no family. But maybe that explained her fierce purpose in giving Dawud links to his paternal as well as maternal cultures.

He was about to ask when Dawud set up a grizzling cry. Instantly Arden was on her feet.

'It's past nap time. I'd better dry him off and let him rest.'

'I'll carry him.' Idris scooped up Dawud and tucked him close. Despite the wetness and the jarring kick of one small heel against his ribs, he enjoyed holding his boy.

They walked together into Dawud's room where Idris reluctantly handed him over. The interlude of intimate communication was over. He should return to his office. It might be their honeymoon but securing peace took precedence, especially now he had a family as well as a nation to protect.

Yet Idris paused, watching mother and son. Again that hard thud resonated through his chest as if his heart beat out of sync.

'Thank you, Arden.'

Her head shot up, her brows furrowing in puzzlement.

'King Dawud was my grandfather. A great leader and revered among my people.' It was a shame his son, Idris's uncle, hadn't ruled in the same mould. 'I'm honoured you named our boy after him, and pleased that you thought to give Dawud such a gift. You could as easily have severed any connection with my country. I appreciate what you've done for him.'

Her eyes rounded, her mouth opening a little before she snapped it shut. 'It seemed only right.'

Idris knew that for many women doing what Arden had would have been a step too far. He admired her for that.

He was discovering Arden was far more than a sexy bed mate and the mother of his son. She might even have the strength and generosity to prove the naysayers wrong and become the Sheikha his kingdom needed. The wife he hadn't realised he wanted till now.

Perhaps marriage wouldn't be nearly the trial he'd imagined.

CHAPTER TEN

ARDEN SMOOTHED THE skirt of her full-length dress. The silvery material was soft as gossamer, the cut amazing. Only the best for the Sheikh's wife.

She stared at the intricately inscribed wedding band on her left hand, proof she really was the Sheikha.

Her mouth quirked. Her life was full of such proofs. She hadn't slept alone since the wedding and had grown used to curling up against Idris's hot, muscled body through the night. She'd almost become accustomed to the hum of arousal that filled her when he looked at her with that particular gleam in his dark eyes.

She'd stopped fretting over the fact she enjoyed the sex, enjoyed being with him. Surely it made sense to accept the perks in this marriage of convenience. Especially when increasingly she caught glimpses of the charming, engaging man she'd known before duty took over Idris's world. That man made her smile even when her day had been exhausting.

A pity she found it far more difficult being royal.

The sight of people bowing before her made her feel a fraud. Even on her visits to schools where the children seemed fascinated by their ruler's foreign wife, Arden felt like an interloper. She enjoyed being with the kids, sharing their smiles and enthusiasm, but all the time she knew they believed her to be someone special when really she was utterly ordinary.

Except for the fact she'd married Idris.

Daily she struggled with the simplest of royal protocols. As for understanding who was who in the complicated hierarchy of regional politics... Arden had given up trying to follow the complex behind-the-scenes machinations and treated everyone with the same courtesy she would have in London. She'd seen raised eyebrows at several gaffes but it was the best she could do. She wasn't bred to this role like Princess Ghizlan.

The thought of Ghizlan made her eyes dart to her dressing room's full length mirror. Arden didn't have Ghizlan's panache but she had to admit that tonight she looked different. With her hair up and wearing a stunning silver couture dress, she looked a far cry from the frazzled single mum who'd attended the royal reception in London in a borrowed dress.

Different enough that Idris would notice?

Of course he'll notice. He doesn't miss anything.

What you mean is, will he appreciate you as he would someone like Princess Ghizlan?

The snide voice made her stiffen. Was she really that pathetic? Idris noticed her. And he was attracted. Their passionate lovemaking proved that.

But Idris made the best of circumstances, as she did. He hadn't chosen her because he loved her, or because she met the qualifications of a well-bred princess. He hadn't really chosen her. She'd been foisted on him by circumstance and scandal.

And still she craved—not his approval—but his admiration. She wanted to be more than an encumbrance or a convenient partner.

Arden stared into the shadowed eyes in the mirror and knew that was bad. She shouldn't need any man's admiration to feel good about herself. This…craving was a weakness. A sign she felt far more than she should for the man she'd married.

Or perhaps, she thought with relief, it was just that things were so different here. She was out of her depth so surely it was natural to crave a sense of belonging, of being appreciated.

A glance out of the window at Zahrat's capital city, a mix of ultra-modern and traditional architecture, reminded her how far she was from home. Everything here, though fascinating and often surprisingly modern and easy, was foreign. Her experience of the world beyond the UK was limited to the single week in Santorini when she'd met and fallen for Idris.

She had so much to learn. No wonder she was floundering, despite the intensive lessons. She hated feeling so out of her depth. It ate at her self-respect.

'Sorry I'm late.' The deep voice made her spin round.

Idris stood in the doorway, in his tailored tuxedo looking scrumptious enough to eat.

Heat radiated across Arden's throat and cheeks as she remembered the way she'd nibbled her way along his body this morning. She'd paused to savour the taste of him till he'd growled impatiently and flung her onto the mattress, imprisoning her with his bulk and driving them both to completion with a series of quick, perfect lunges that reminded her again how very good he was at sex, how experienced, especially compared with her.

'Are you okay?' His brow knitted and he stepped closer. 'I'll be by your side all evening. There's nothing to worry about.'

Arden forced her mind away from the delights of his naked body. 'Of course there isn't. Who'd get nervous about a royal reception for several hundred VIPs?'

Idris smiled and her heart gave that little shivery beat. The man had too much charisma, especially with that hint of a laugh in his eyes. 'Most of them will be more nervous than you. Besides, all you need to do is smile and be yourself. They'll be charmed.'

Sure. As if the local glitterati were interested in the ramblings of a London florist whose passions, apart from her son and her sexy husband, were gardening, tennis and curling up with a good book.

'I've brought you this. I thought you might like to wear it tonight.' He held up a box of royal-blue leather, stamped with ornate gilt work. Arden recognised it. The diamond and pearl necklaces she'd worn at their wedding had been lifted reverentially from similar boxes.

'That treasury of yours must be enormous,' she murmured, forcing a smile to cover her nerves. The value of the pieces she'd worn at the wedding had only added to her tension. What if she'd damaged them?

'It's big enough. Remind me to take you to look. You could pick out some pieces you like.'

Arden couldn't imagine it. She wasn't the sort to wear pigeon's egg rubies to show off her newly manicured hands.

'Aren't you going to open it?'

Her eyes snapped to his. She thought she read excitement there. But she must have imagined it—a second later and the impression was gone as he glanced at his watch. It was time they made their appearance.

Taking a deep breath, Arden lifted the tiny gold latch then raised the lid. Whatever she'd been about to say disintegrated as she gasped, barely able to take in what she saw.

'You like it?'

Arden shook her head. Surely it couldn't be real.

'Of course it's real.' Had she spoken aloud?

A large, square hand plucked the exquisite choker necklace from its nest of oyster satin and lifted it, dazzling her.

The piece was about two inches wide, diamonds and platinum creating a delicate tracery of leaves that sparkled outrageously. Above and below it was edged with what looked like ribbon but was actually square cut green stones she guessed were emeralds. The necklace secured at the back and at the front it dipped gracefully towards a single huge faceted emerald drop.

'I've never seen anything like it,' she croaked. It should belong to an empress.

'Here, let me.' Idris stepped behind her and she felt the cool weight of it around her throat, the pendant heavy against her skin while his fingers deftly closed the clasp at her nape. 'Take a look. It goes perfectly with what you're wearing.'

Arden was still in shock and it affected her hearing. To her ears Idris's voice sounded strangely hoarse. And the grip of his hands as he turned her towards the mirror seemed to dig in too hard.

She lifted her head and stared.

'Well?' Idris cleared his throat over unfamiliar tightness. 'Do you like it?'

'I don't know what to say.' In the mirror Arden's eyes were huge, but she didn't smile.

Why didn't she react? In the past generous gifts to lovers had been received with enthusiasm.

But this was different. *She* was different. He'd never had a lover so unconcerned with his prestige and wealth. Arden tried hard to fit in with life at court but he suspected she wasn't impressed by its pomp.

Which made him wonder how she felt about *him*. It niggled that, except when they were naked, he found it hard to read her thoughts.

He'd commissioned this personally with her in mind. He'd seen some preliminary work by a renowned jeweller and immediately imagined it gracing Arden's slender throat. He'd never before had something made specifically for any woman. Was that why he was eager for her reaction?

It looked superb. Regal but feminine. Elegant but incredibly sexy. So sexy he wanted to see her wear it and nothing else. He wanted to ignore the guests waiting in the Hall of a Thousand Pillars and make urgent love to her.

Then make slow, thorough love to her all over again.

He was on fire and not just because she looked spectacular in silk and emeralds. He always burned for her. Even when she wore old clothes to finger paint with Dawud. Especially when she wore those tight jeans…

Idris forced his hands from her bare arms, looking over her shoulder at her reflection in the glass. *His wife. His queen.*

She was beautiful.

'Say you like it.' The words jerked out, appallingly needy, as if he craved approval. It was an unfamiliar feeling, one that disturbed him.

'I like it.' Their eyes met in the mirror and his doubts fled. What he read in her face, the softening warmth and wonder, were everything he could want.

It reminded him of her ardent passion. Every time they had sex she made him feel more than the man he'd been before. He was rapidly becoming addicted to that radiant pleasure.

This was the first time Arden had regarded him with that glowing wonder when they weren't having sex. Idris wrapped an arm around her waist, tugging her back against him, revelling in the way she fitted so perfectly.

'Though I'm not sure it's really me,' she whispered. 'I'm more a noodle sort of girl.' Her mouth twisted wryly in that self-effacing way and Idris recognised the reference to the bangle she and Dawud had made one day out of dry pasta.

'Believe me, it's you.' She mightn't be the most classically beautiful woman in the world, but Arden had a vibrant loveliness all her own. 'You look spectacular.'

Soft colour washed her cheeks. 'Not as spectacular as you.'

'Even without diamonds?' He pretended to preen and was delighted when she giggled.

Two months of marriage and he'd discovered her smiles could change his mood in an instant. Each one felt like a gift to be savoured. More and more he found himself responding, teasing and laughing, living in the moment instead of always focused on work.

Why was Arden's warmth and enthusiasm so potent? He put it down to the fact it was easier to live with a woman who was upbeat and practical, ready to meet him halfway. He'd discovered marriage far less difficult than expected, if he didn't count the continuing fallout over his choice of bride. Though even that was fading as diplomacy, frantic hard work and his bride's refreshing ways worked their magic.

'Diamonds would be overkill with that dinner jacket.' Her smooth brow furrowed. Her fingers went tentatively to the emerald resting just below her collarbone. 'You're sure about this? I can't help feeling nervous wearing something so expensive and beautiful.'

Idris had never heard any woman express such a sentiment. Arden continued to surprise him.

'I'm sure. You can pretend it's made of pasta if that makes it easier.'

She grinned and a shaft of warmth shot straight through him. 'I might just do that.'

'Come on, Princess.' He turned and held out his arm.

He couldn't describe the feeling inside when she smiled up at him and slipped her arm through his. Satisfaction, triumph, pride. None quite captured the unfamiliar blast of delight he experienced as he swept out of the room with Arden on his arm.

Arden was flagging after the initial round of introductions but gamely kept her chin up. How Idris managed so many handshakes, so many bows and introductions from people all eager to make an impression, she didn't know. Her muscles ached from fatigue, even though she'd taken Ghizlan's advice and worn beautiful shoes that were still comfortable and not skyscraper tall.

She wished Ghizlan was here. It would have been comforting to have a friend on her side. People were generally pleasant, except for those few older men who always regarded her stonily as if her presence was a catastrophe. Arden drew in a slow breath, reminding herself acceptance would take time.

Nevertheless it was tough keeping up the image of royal correctness. Formality didn't come naturally to Arden.

Ghizlan had understood her total inexperience. There'd been no need to pretend with her and that had been liberating. Against the odds they'd bonded over the fiasco in London. Ghizlan had texted answers to questions about dress codes and etiquette, along with scurrilously funny anecdotes about ceremonial disasters, for months now. But in the last few days there'd been nothing. Not since her initial response to Arden's sympathy on her father's unexpected death.

Ghizlan had returned home and it was no surprise she had no time for messages. Idris said there was some question over who would succeed Ghizlan's father as Sheikh. Ghizlan would be busy with that and—

'Excuse me, Sire. I must talk with you.'

Arden blinked, stirred from distraction by the voice of the palace steward. The line of people being presented had petered out so she and Idris stood a little apart from the throng, on the royal dais. Two thrones inlaid with gold and precious stones dominated the area and she'd deliberately turned her back on them. Silly to be overawed by some furniture but they, like the eye-watering perfection of the necklace she felt every time she swallowed, reminded her she was an imposter here.

'Can't it wait?' Idris matched his voice to the steward's low tone.

'I'm afraid not, Your Highness. I would have done something about it before but you asked me to leave tonight's arrangements to my staff—'

'Because I entrusted you with the celebrations to open the new city hall and convention centre next week. I value your expertise to bring it off in style.'

'I pride myself it will be a success, sir. But in my absence there's been a…regrettable error of judgement. A problem with the banqueting hall I've just discovered.'

'A problem? It was in perfect condition yesterday. Has it been damaged?'

A tingling began between Arden's shoulder blades. A tingling that skittered down her spine and wound into her belly, unsettling her already nervous stomach. She swung around to meet the palace steward's eyes just before he dragged his gaze back to Idris.

The tingling became a wash of foreboding, stirring nausea. Had she erred again? And tonight of all nights, when she'd been at such pains to complete her royal duties with grace and decorum?

'Not damage as such, Your Highness. If I'd been here it would have been rectified immediately. Unfortunately my second in charge, though competent, isn't as familiar with the way things must be done.'

The old man's eyes flickered but didn't meet hers. Yet Arden knew instantly he was remembering the times they'd clashed. The day when, thin-lipped, he'd warned her that using an ancient mosaic-floored corridor for games with Dawud was inadvisable. And that allowing a group of visiting schoolchildren into one of the palace courtyards might not only damage national treasures but show disrespect for royal tradition.

His manner intimated that disregard for the riches surrounding them was only what he'd expect of an outsider who had no concept of Zahrati custom and sensibilities.

'I'm afraid it's probably my fault,' Arden said, her voice defensively brusque. She was tired of being on the back foot, continually reminded of the many ways she didn't measure up as a royal spouse. Not that Idris ever said a word. But others, like the steward, were always sure to tell her.

'Your fault?' Idris smiled and heat danced through her, reminding her of the strange intimacy between them when he'd given her the necklace. Of the sense, for a second or two, that maybe she was wrong and there was more to their marriage than convenience and necessity.

The steward shuffled his feet and the idea shattered.

'I suspect the problem relates to today's visitors. Am I right?'

She met the steward's guarded stare with outward confidence. She mightn't like the man, might even believe he was deliberately difficult, but she had no intention of showing her horror that once more she was in the wrong. First there'd been the contretemps when an elderly lady had curtsied to her and Arden had impulsively helped her rise when it seemed her knees had locked. How was she to know that touching a stranger at court without invitation was a shocking misdemeanour?

Since then there'd been several *faux pas*. The night she'd used a fruit spoon instead of the purpose-designed sorbet spoon from the vast array of gold cutlery was the least of her dining mistakes. The reception where palace staff, eager in the knowledge their new Sheikha had a reputation for liking flowers, had installed numerous floral arrangements complete with trailing jasmine. Sadly Arden hadn't thought to warn them she was allergic to the scent and she'd spent the evening sneezing through every speech.

'I met with some school groups today.' She turned to Idris, her smile perfunctory. 'You said it was all right to have them here.'

Since her visit to Leila, the girl who'd offered her a bouquet in the street, Arden had been invited to several schools. Seeing the enthusiasm of both children and adults, Arden had sought Idris's approval to invite some school groups to the palace. Today goggle-eyed children had taken in the grandeur of the reception rooms while teachers expounded on the palace's historic treasures.

Another reason the steward disapproved of her. Previously only VIPs saw the palace interior. In

Zahrat there was traditionally little direct contact between the royal family and their subjects.

'I'm sorry,' Idris murmured. 'I didn't ask you how the visits went.'

'Excellent. I thought it a success, and so did the teachers. The children were excited but very well behaved.' Arden glimpsed the steward's impatience and felt her heart sink. Obviously something had gone wrong. She hoped some priceless ornament hadn't been damaged.

'So what's the problem?' Idris turned to the steward.

'It's the banqueting hall, Sire. I just returned to the palace and saw the room had been *decorated* in a way that made it unfit for tonight's formal dinner.' He almost groaned his horror. 'I told the staff to fix it immediately but was informed the Sheikha had said the...decorations were to remain until she directed otherwise.' His glare said what he thought of that.

Over the steward's shoulder she saw staff opening the doors into the adjoining banqueting room. Arden's pulse fluttered as she remembered how that room had looked today when the children visited. Laughter bubbled inside but it died as she watched the first of the exquisitely dressed VIPs pass through the open doors. They all looked so suave and important.

'I'm sorry.' She swung around to Idris. 'It's my fault. The younger children brought gifts as a thank you for their visit and I said we should display them. Some of the staff seemed eager to remove the decorations as soon as possible but I didn't want to disappoint the kids by taking them down while they were in the building. I told the staff to leave them till I instructed they be removed.' Except later she'd forgotten.

'That's the problem?' Idris frowned. 'Gifts from children in the banqueting hall?'

The steward stepped closer. 'No fault attaches to the children or teachers. The gifts were a sign of appreciation. But sadly they are inappropriate in such a majestic setting. Especially given tonight's formal diplomatic dinner.'

The man didn't look at Arden, but something inside her shrank. Clearly if fault lay anywhere it was with her.

Once she'd have thought the old man overreacted, but she knew Idris had faced a firestorm because of their marriage. He'd worked tirelessly to rectify damage from the scandal. Tonight was a major part of his campaign to have his nobody of a foreign wife accepted. The place was filled with diplomats and VIPs.

Had she sabotaged it? Arden felt sick at the thought.

'Thank you, Selim, for the warning. We'll manage from here. I'm sure it will be all right.' Idris took her arm, holding it high as he led her off the dais and towards the crowd disappearing into the banqueting room.

Arden's stomach felt like lead but she had no choice but to tilt her head up, fix on a smile and follow his lead.

Idris paused in the doorway to the vast banqueting room and tightened his lips to repress a broad grin. Elegant guests milled around tables laid for a seven course banquet. Surrounding them were pillared walls of shell-pink marble carved by master craftsmen generations ago. And blooming on the priceless marble was a lopsided, improbable field of bright blossom.

Huge paper flowers in purple, orange, sunburst-yellow and even sky-blue crowded the surfaces in ragged, enthusiastic abandon. He spied names written in crayon on the leaves.

Idris paced further into the room, Arden with him, her hand cold in his. Was she so nervous of the official reception? She'd done marvellously through the lengthy introductions, greeting people with a charm and warmth that came naturally to her. She was a people person and a welcome breath of fresh air.

'It's fine,' he said under his breath, pressing her hand reassuringly. 'Nothing to worry about.'

Her fingers twitched in his hold and she nodded, but her smile looked fixed. Damn Selim for bustling in, making a fuss and upsetting Arden.

That was why Idris had put the steward in charge of the city hall opening. It was an excuse to get him out of the palace. Idris knew he took any chance to show her up.

He led Arden towards a cluster of lopsided sunflowers. 'I've never seen the place so festive.'

She looked up, eyes wide. 'Not even at our wedding banquet?' she murmured.

Idris remembered the cloth of gold swags at each entrance, the garlands of exotic lilies intertwined with crystal and pearls on each table. 'These are simple but they're gifts from the heart.' He preferred them to the formal opulence of the wedding.

He turned, smiling and raising his voice so the guests could hear. 'I hope you enjoy the decorations for our meal tonight. You all know my wife's interest in our children and her visits to local schools. These are gifts brought by students from those schools. I think you'll agree they show great enthusiasm and creativity.'

There was a murmur of voices and a few nods though some of the guests still looked bemused.

Idris caught the eye of the Minister of Education, one of the government leaders who'd actually been eager for the modernisation Idris had been leading.

The Minister inclined his head. 'Encouraging our children in art as well as the sciences is traditional in Zahrat. It's good to see that continuing with the personal support of our new Sheikha.' He smiled and Idris heard Arden's snatched breath. She hadn't expected the compliment.

The realisation angered Idris.

He'd been so frantic dealing with the fallout from his sudden marriage and its impact on both the peace treaty and his own position. Becoming a husband and father had distracted him too. He'd known Arden faced difficulties but hadn't realised she felt so vulnerable. Guilt hit.

He pulled her close, abandoning any pretence of royal dignity as he wrapped his arm around her waist, ignoring the way she stiffened.

'Come,' he ordered, his voice rough with barely concealed annoyance at himself. He should have done more, he saw now, to ease her into her new responsibilities. He should never have left it to his staff. 'Tell me about these flowers. Particularly this one.' He injected a light-hearted note. 'It seems, intriguingly, to resemble a camel.'

Tense she might be, but Arden was quick. 'That's because it's a camel, despite the petals. The little boy...'

'Ali?' Idris tilted his head to read the name written on one knobbly camel's leg.

'That's it.' Her smile looked almost natural now. 'Ali confessed he didn't like flowers. He likes camels so that's the shape he cut out. But when he heard the class had been asked to make flowers for me because I liked them, he compromised by putting petals on his camel. That's why the hump droops.'

Idris chuckled, imagining the scene, and there was a ripple of laughter as guests moved to inspect the work.

By the time they sat down to dinner, Arden, sitting opposite him with an ambassador on one side and the Minister for Education on the other, looked almost relaxed. Her smile wasn't radiant, but as the meal progressed the horrible tension he'd felt in her dissipated and she charmed her companions with her ability to listen and her direct questions.

Idris had been right. Arden would make an excellent sheikha. Just as she was a superb mother. And as a wife—

She lifted her head abruptly, catching him staring. Pink stained her cheeks as their eyes met. By the time she looked away Idris found himself impatiently counting the time till they could be alone together.

CHAPTER ELEVEN

IT WAS WELL past midnight when they reached their private apartment. Arden was exhausted. Every muscle groaned from being held taut so long. Her jaw ached from smiling and a stress headache throbbed in time with the beat of her pulse.

Idris had handled the situation suavely, turning what could have been embarrassing into an opportunity to promote his agenda for improved education.

Yet the fact remained he'd had to cover for her slip up. Again.

Everyone made mistakes. It was just that hers were always in a glaring spotlight of public disapproval. And after months of marriage she was making as many as ever.

Arden had known she wasn't suited for the role of royal wife. How long before her shortcomings created a rift between Idris and those who supported him?

She knew he was popular—he'd gathered support through sheer hard work and the positive results of every hard-won reform. But she also knew there were traditionalists in high places horrified at the scandal surrounding his marriage. And her unsuitability as his wife. People who could make trouble, not just for her but for Idris and all he was trying to do.

She'd been on tenterhooks tonight, trying to remember the correct forms of address and so many other minutiae of Zahrati custom. She'd been congratulating herself on getting through the first part of her trial by etiquette when the steward brought his news.

Nor had she missed her husband's set expression when he'd entered the banqueting hall and discovered its elegance marred by wonky paper flowers. Idris hadn't been impressed.

'I'm really sorry about tonight.' She crossed to the dressing table, pulling out hairpins, stifling a sigh as the tight, elegant coiffure disintegrated into waves around her shoulders.

'Sorry?'

Arden put the hairpins down, hating that her fingers shook. Keeping up the appearance of ease all evening, while her stomach roiled with nerves, had taken its toll.

Abruptly she turned, only to find Idris right behind her. He grabbed her shoulders before she could walk into him, his dark eyes peering straight into her soul.

Arden's heart kicked. Even weary and despondent, desire shivered through her. Her need for him was constant, unrelenting. He didn't love her and her love for Idris had died in the years she'd believed he'd abandoned her, yet her yearning for him only seemed to grow.

If she wasn't careful he'd take over her life even more than he had already. She'd lost her home, her job, her independence. She couldn't afford to lose any more. She needed to be able to stand up for herself and her son.

Arden sidestepped, dragging in a quick, relieved breath when he dropped his hands.

'I'm sorry about the banqueting hall. That was my fault. I should have had the artwork taken down hours ago.'

She just hadn't thought of it. Straight after the school visits she'd met a delegation of women who'd travelled two days to present their new Sheikha with gifts they'd prepared themselves: delicious attar of rose scent and exquisitely woven stoles. Then there'd been an afternoon crammed with language lessons and appointments, including one with a stylist who'd clearly been challenged by Arden's riotous hair. There had been barely enough time to see Dawud before his bed time.

'Don't fret, Arden. It's not a problem.' Idris's soothing voice only stirred her guilt. She knew tonight could have been a disaster. 'Our guests loved the decorations.'

He stepped into her line of vision but didn't touch her. Arden was glad. She wanted distance, didn't she?

Except, stupidly, she also wanted to lean her tired head on her husband's broad shoulder.

'Only because you turned it into something they could relate to. If not for that…' She shook her head, remembering the initially stunned looks from their guests and the palace steward's outrage.

'You're worrying too much. You saw the reaction Ali's camel got.' Idris's chuckle wrapped around her like balm on a wound and the gleam in his eyes tugged at her. 'Maybe we should add Dawud's finger painting to the display. What do you say? I think the boy's got real talent.'

Despite herself Arden grinned, thinking of Dawud's latest picture of the three of them, all heads and spindly legs. And how Idris had joined in the painting, teasingly threatening to daub her nose with red paint when she dared to critique his efforts.

'Our guests were delighted by the art. It's exactly the down-to-earth touch I want. The palace has been cut off from the people too long. Maybe we should expand those school visits into a regular programme.'

'Your steward will love that,' she murmured, trying and failing to picture the old man smiling as children invaded the Hall of a Thousand Pillars.

Instantly Idris sobered. 'He won't be here. Tomorrow he'll be relieved of his duties.'

Arden gazed, stunned at Idris's stern expression. It gave the lie to his assurance that tonight had been a storm in a teacup.

'I told you—' she stepped near, inhaling the scent of sandalwood and spicy male '—that was down to me. It wasn't his fault.'

Idris shook his head. 'I'm not worried about the banqueting hall. What concerns me is that Selim made a ridiculous fuss about it in front of you. I know he's a stickler for the old ways and he makes you nervous with his fussing. That's why he's been working outside the palace.'

Arden's jaw dropped. 'Because of *me*?' She was torn between dismay that her discomfort had led to such drastic action and glowing warmth because Idris had tried to make things easy for her.

His mouth tightened, his expression austere. 'You are my wife and his queen. If he makes you uneasy he goes. Permanently.'

Arden blinked. Before her eyes her husband had morphed into the proud autocrat she remembered from London. It struck her that she hadn't glimpsed that man lately.

Idris might get distracted by politics but she enjoyed being with him. He was patient and gentle with Dawud, passionate with her. Good company, she realised, sometimes teasing but never dismissing her concerns. Never aloof.

The autocratic warrior King hadn't made an appearance in ages. To her surprise she wasn't fazed by him any more. Now she understood that expression was Idris determined to do what he believed was right, even if difficult. He'd moved on from the carefree, thoughtless man she'd once known. She discovered she actually liked this man better—the complex mix of strength and honesty, of decency as well as passion and humour.

'You can't dismiss him.'

'I won't have him making you nervous. He undermines your confidence.'

Arden stared, flummoxed that Idris had noticed what she'd taken care to hide. 'How do you know? Most of the time you're not around when I'm with him.'

One sleek jet-black brow tilted high. 'I notice everything about you, Arden.' She had the strangest sensation of his words echoing endlessly within her. His stare was intense, as if he read her deepest secrets. He lifted a hand, stroking her cheek in a butterfly touch that resonated right to her core.

Arden felt the weight of something powerful between them, something she couldn't name. Then he spoke and the instant shattered.

'He unsettles you. He'll leave tomorrow.'

She caught Idris's wrist. 'No. Don't do it.'

'I won't have you undermined.'

Arden's lips curved in a tight smile as she recognised that her husband's support bolstered her flagging determination. It was *she* who'd made a mountain out of a molehill tonight. She'd let herself be led by Selim, fretting over something that, now she considered properly, was a minor glitch.

'He works hard and he's good at what he does. He doesn't deserve to lose his job.' Still Idris looked unconvinced. 'I can cope. I *prefer* to.'

'There's no need. Let me do this for you.' The look in his eyes made her chest tighten as she forgot to breathe. She dropped her hand from his. She wasn't used to being looked after. It was nice but scary too…unfamiliar.

'I know you're trying to help but it would be wrong. He *does* fuss and make me feel like an uneducated barbarian—' Idris's breath hissed. 'But he's retiring soon.'

'In thirteen months.' Idris must have checked. For some reason that lightened her mood. He really had given this thought, and not just tonight.

'That will give him time to train his replacement. Besides, I can learn a lot from him.'

Still Idris frowned.

'Did I ever tell you about my first boss, when I began as a florist?'

He shook his head.

'She must have liked something about me since she hired me but to begin with I never did anything right, even sweeping the cuttings off the floor.'

'She sounds like a tartar.'

'She was. But she was also passionate about

what she did and expected the best. She insisted everything I did was the best it could be.' Arden shook her head. 'I remember rewiring the first bridal bouquet I did for her until I got it just right. But in the end I was glad she was so picky because I acquired the skills and confidence to cope, no matter how demanding the work.'

Something like a smile danced in Idris's eyes. 'That's why you'd rather keep our palace perfectionist?'

Arden lifted her hands, palm up. 'He's here and has an encyclopaedic knowledge of royal ritual and custom. I might as well make the most of him, even if he does make me want to gnash my teeth sometimes.'

Idris's laugh curled round her like tendrils of silk, caressing tight muscles. Even the dull headache diminished a fraction.

'On one condition.' The laughter faded. 'If you change your mind, or if I catch a hint of disapproval from him, he's out.'

'Agreed.' Yet still Idris didn't look totally sold.

'I'll be fine, really.' Surprisingly, after the doubts that had dogged her so long, she actually believed it. Something had changed tonight and it made her more than ever determined to make a go of this official side of their marriage.

The private part was already working well.

Well? She'd never imagined anything so good. Dawud was thriving. Idris was a caring, involved father and as a husband…she couldn't ask for more. He was considerate, passionate and respectful of her needs.

It would be too easy to believe their union was real, a marriage of hearts as well as minds. Alarms sounded in Arden's head. This was no match made in heaven.

She shifted back a fraction, making her point. 'I appreciate you supporting me. But it's important that I stand on my own two feet. It's the only way I know.'

Freshly showered, Idris flicked off all the lights except a bedside lamp and slipped naked between the sheets. Arden was in her bathroom and he'd been tempted to seduce her there. Except he remembered how she'd trembled with tiredness as they talked. He'd seen her tension and guessed her head ached. She'd slitted her eyes against the light and more than once lifted her hand to her forehead, massaging absently.

When her bathroom door opened, predictably his body tightened with desire. Her hair was a frothing, rich gleam around pale shoulders and her lacy nightgown clung to that delicious body the way his hands itched to.

Day after day, night after night, he couldn't get enough of Arden. A heavy schedule, the burden of renegotiating a new agreement with neighbouring kingdoms, all the concerns of a ruler for his country, couldn't distract from this hunger. It puzzled him how passion kept growing, intensifying rather than diminishing with familiarity.

She slipped into bed and he saw the shadows beneath her eyes, the furrow of pain on her brow. Regret rose. He could convince her into sex. She'd enjoy it—he'd make sure of it. But Arden had had enough for one night.

'Here, move closer.' He lifted the sheet, encouraging her to his side of the bed.

'I'm tired, Idris.' Even so, he saw the way her gaze dipped down his bare body.

'I know, *habibti*. You can just sleep.'

He'd never been fond of sleeping tangled up against anyone. The exception had always been Arden. When they'd first met he'd put it down to exhaustion, after wearing themselves to the point of oblivion with sex. These past months, though, Idris had discovered he *liked* holding her as they rested. It felt...satisfying.

'It doesn't look like it's sleep you have in mind.'

His erection throbbed in response to her stare and Idris hauled her close. Instantly his body hardened still further, eager for intimacy. The wriggle of her hip then her buttocks against his arousal as she turned to spoon against him, tore the air from his lungs.

'Stop twitching,' he growled.

Was that a tiny, breathless laugh? He slid his arm around her and cupped her breast, his thumb moving in a deliberate, slow caress of her peaking nipple.

'Idris!' The sibilant was soft and drawn out, just the way he liked her saying his name. A grim smile tightened his features as he tried to ignore the pleas of his body.

He distracted himself with the fact she'd called him Idris. In the first weeks of marriage Shakil had been the name on her lips when she urged him on in the throes of passion, or when she cried out in climax. It had felt oddly as if she betrayed him with another man. Shakil might only have been his younger self but Idris had wanted Arden in the present, making love to *him*, not a memory.

He hadn't heard the name Shakil for more than a month. That pleased him, satisfying a proprietorial side to his nature he'd never before recognised.

'Shh. Relax.'

'How can I relax when you do that?'

Sighing, Idris released her breast, sliding his hand down lace and silk to splay over her belly.

He focused on controlling his breathing and found his thoughts turning to the idea of Arden carrying his baby. He'd missed so much—her pregnancy and Dawud's early years. The idea of sharing such experiences appealed, the idea of her pregnant again stirring impulses he was trying to stifle.

'You're twitching,' she murmured.

'You're distracting me.' He only had to catch her

light orange blossom scent and he was distracted. 'You said you were used to looking after yourself. Why is that?' Talking would take his mind off his body's torture. Besides, he wanted to know.

'I'm used to being alone.'

Idris found that hard to believe. But then he'd been stunned all those years ago in Greece to discover Arden was a virgin. 'Are all the men in England blind?'

She huffed out a laugh and the movement made him grit his teeth. He was sensitive—too sensitive.

'You're such a smooth talker.'

'Only stating the truth. Surely in all these years there was someone…with you.' Idris chose his words carefully.

'I *told* you; your cousin was just a friend. A good friend and, after a time, my landlord. But that's all.'

'No need to get het up. I believe you. But in four years there must have been someone.'

'Must there?' She paused and Idris realised he had second thoughts. He didn't want to know about her love life after all. 'Well, you're wrong. There was no one.'

'No one?' It barely seemed possible. Yet elation rose in a soaring wave. It shouldn't matter. She'd been a free agent, like him. Yet the idea of Arden with other men—

'Don't sound so surprised. I was pregnant to start with and later…' Later, what? Surely he didn't expect her to say she'd pined for him. Not when she'd thought he'd dumped her. 'Later there were barely enough hours in the day for everything that had to be done, looking after Dawud, working, scrimping to make ends meet.'

Guilt tightened his gut. His splayed hand pressed her close. 'You don't have to worry about being alone ever again.' He'd take care of them both. They were his responsibility. More, he *wanted* to look after Arden and Dawud.

Instead of easing in his embrace, Arden stiffened as if she might pull free of his hold.

'What is it?' Sixth sense told him he'd hit a nerve.

'Nothing. I'd like to sleep now.' But she held herself rigid, her breathing short. She was hiding something or, he amended, protecting herself. From him? The idea was like biting down on a crisp apple, only to taste the sourness of decay.

'I mean it, Arden. You have me now, as well as Dawud.' Surely she didn't think he'd abandon them? Not after he'd gone to such lengths to marry her?

'Yes.' Yet her voice didn't convince.

'Why did you make such a point earlier about the fact you were used to standing up for yourself?' She'd made similar comments in London.

'I told you; it's what I've always done.'

Silence. Not the companionable silence of a few minutes ago, but an edgy wariness. He'd bet her eyes were wide open. He felt tension hum through her.

'Me too,' he said slowly, deciding against another direct query. 'I was an only child. That makes a difference, don't you think?'

She shrugged. 'I suppose so.'

'I wasn't close to my parents. Well,' he amended, 'to my mother when I was very young. But she died when I was just a kid.'

'Really? How old were you?'

'Four.'

'I'm sorry.'

'It was a long time ago. I had my father and aunts and uncles, plus my cousin, Hamid.'

'Your father brought you up?'

Idris felt his lips tighten. 'My father wasn't a hands-on dad. He had other interests.' Like seducing other men's wives. His father's relentless pursuit of pleasure and string of conquests hadn't made him warm or contented.

Idris had started out the same. Not seducing other men's wives, but sowing plenty of wild oats.

'I was brought up by tutors and members of my uncle's court. There was a focus on honour and duty.' Probably to counteract the wayward tendencies of the males in his family. 'How about you?'

'Sorry?'

'Who brought you up? I know your parents died but I have no idea when.'

Seconds stretched before she answered. 'They died when I was six.'

'Both?' His voice was sharp with surprise.

'It was a car accident. They died at the scene of the crash.'

Something about her tone made his nape prickle. 'You were there?'

'In the back seat.'

'Oh, Arden.' He wrapped himself tighter around her, tugging her back against him. 'I'm so sorry.'

'Like in your case, it was a long time ago.'

'But still tragic.' And difficult for her even now. It was there in her too flat voice and the way she held herself. 'It's young to lose your family.'

'Yes,' she said dully. 'I was losing them anyway but death is so final.' She drew a deep breath, her ribs expanding against his chest. 'They used to argue a lot. That night in the car, they thought I was asleep and they were at it again. Dad said he was getting a divorce and they were fighting over who'd have me. Dad didn't want to take me and Mum was upset, saying she couldn't manage alone. In the end they didn't have to worry.'

What could he say to that? Idris didn't try. He pressed his lips to her hair, gently reminding her of his presence.

'Did you have any family at all? Aunts and uncles?' He, at least, had had extended family when he'd lost his mother.

Arden shook her head. 'I went into foster care.'

'I'm sorry.' Idris couldn't believe he'd never thought to learn her history. Surely it had shaped Arden. Shame was a hot blade in his belly. He'd been too busy with other things to try understanding the woman he'd married.

'Don't be. It was okay most of the time.'

'And the rest of the time?' He'd heard appalling stories about defenceless, vulnerable children.

'Truly, it was okay. I was with one family for years. They treated me like their own little girl and I was happy. They were very kind.' Yet sadness lingered in her voice.

'But you left them?' he guessed.

'They planned to adopt me. They couldn't have children and wanted to keep me as theirs. But right at the end, before everything could be finalised, a miracle happened.' Her voice was matter-of-fact, as if she recited words supplied by someone else. It made his chest clench. 'They discovered they were expecting, not just one baby but twins.'

Arden drew a deep breath. 'They were nice people and upset they'd led me on only to disappoint me. They just couldn't afford three children or find space for that many. It wasn't anything personal.'

'Of course not.' Yet he wanted to find them and screw their necks for the pain they'd caused her.

Now he had some inkling of why Arden was so adamant about standing up for herself. Had there ever been anyone she could rely on long term?

She'd witnessed her parents squabbling about who'd have to take her as they tore their family apart. Then she'd lost them both in horrific circumstances. Years later she'd lost the second secure home she'd known in a way guaranteed to break any child's heart.

And don't forget your part in her life. You seduced her and walked away without a backward glance. She thought you'd deliberately dumped her, abandoned her without a thought that she might be pregnant.

It hadn't been deliberate but he hadn't considered possible consequences. He hadn't made sure she was okay. He'd been too wrapped up in Zahrat and his own concerns.

He tightened his arms about her but now there was nothing sexual about his embrace. 'I'm here and I'm not leaving,' he whispered against her hair, shutting his eyes as her sweet fragrance filled his senses. 'I'm not walking away from this marriage. You and Dawud are safe with me.'

He'd make her happy. Make sure she never regretted marrying him.

CHAPTER TWELVE

A SHARP RAP on his open office door made Idris look up from his computer. Ashar, his aide, was already crossing the room, his expression shadowed. Foreboding streaked through Idris at that look.

'What is it?' Some new disaster. The treaty?

'Everything's under control; they're both safe.' Which meant it was Arden and Dawud.

Idris surged to his feet. 'Define *under control*. What's happened now?' It wasn't that Arden attracted trouble. It was more that her limited knowledge of Zahrat and her enthusiasm sometimes led her into unexpected situations.

Not just her. The palace was awash with children's artwork: flowers, animals, even a few dragons and a sea monster. Since news of the decorated banqueting hall got out, schools across the country had sent contributions for display. The Ministry of Education had quickly brought forward reforms to encourage creativity and innovation in schools to take advantage of public interest. A display of the art was planned for the new city hall, along with awards for teaching innovation—all part of the agenda to increase school attendance.

'You're sure they're both safe?' Idris leaned forward on fisted hands.

'They're fine. Their bodyguard is following them.'

The steely grip of tension in Idris's shoulders and spine didn't ease. 'Following? That implies they don't know where they're going.'

'That's why I came to see you. To check if you know of the Sheikha's plans for the afternoon.'

Idris shook his head. 'A visit to a community playgroup with Dawud then back here.' Idris had thought long and hard about letting his son accompany Arden on the visit, but she'd been so eager and so persuasive. He'd wondered if Arden was lonely for the company of women her own age, young mothers with children. Her life was so different here from what it had been in London.

'They went to the playgroup, then they walked to the covered market where they bought food.'

Food? When they had a galley of chefs busy in the palace? It didn't make sense. There'd been no mention of a trip to the market this morning. 'Where are they now?'

'Driving the inland highway. The Sheikha is driving herself.'

Idris frowned. It was usual for Arden to have a driver as well as bodyguards. Mainly as a symbol of her status, since the threat level in Zahrat was virtually non-existent. But there was still the possibility of danger.

A new thought struck. That highway led to Zahrat's interior mountain range and to the airport. Arden wouldn't head to the mountains so late in the day. But the airport?

He rounded his desk, heading for the door. 'Get me the chopper *now*, and a line to the head of security.'

The *whoomp, whoomp, whoomp* of a helicopter split the late-afternoon quiet. Arden looked up, wondering where it was heading, but the endless blue sky was clear and the sound ceased. It must have landed nearby. She recalled Idris saying they used helicopters for mercy hospital flights. Perhaps someone had been injured on the highway.

'Mama. Look at fiss.' Dawud dragged her attention back to the pond where ornamental fish darted, glinting in the sunlight.

'Yes, darling. Lovely fish.' She grinned at her son's fascination with water—an unexpected trait in the son of a desert sheikh. Back at the palace he loved nothing better than paddling in the reflection pools. It was time she taught him to swim. She'd feel better when she knew he could keep himself afloat.

'Come on, our picnic's ready.' She patted the soft grass beside her in the dappled shade.

'Bye-bye, fiss.' He waved solemnly to the fish then trotted over to plop down beside her.

In the same instant swift movement in her peripheral vision made her twist around.

'Idris!' He strode across the garden courtyard, his expression harsh. Behind him she saw two men in black, her security detail, melting back behind the golden stone arches of this ancient palace. 'What are you doing here?'

'I could ask you the same thing.' He sounded different, his accent pronounced, his tone terse.

He looked different too.

Almost, she realised in shock, like the arrogant man she remembered from London. The autocratic warrior prince who expected instant obedience. His expression was stern, almost harsh.

'Baba!' Dawud was on his feet in a moment, hurrying towards his father, arms upstretched. Idris scooped him up in one easy movement, swinging him so high he giggled.

Arden watched the carved lines of Idris's face ease, his face creasing into a smile as Dawud wrapped his arms around his neck, burrowing close. Her heart leapt hard against her breastbone, seeing her son's unquestioning love for the big man who'd been a stranger till a few months ago, and such tenderness in Idris's expression. She'd done the right thing for Dawud, marrying Idris.

His gaze caught hers again and something hot and potent shivered through her.

'What are you doing here?'

'Having a picnic.' She waved to the packets she was unwrapping—dates and apricots, flat bread, soft goat's cheese, nuts and her favourite tiny pastries filled with pistachios and drenched in sweet syrup. 'Would you like to join us? I wasn't expecting to see you till tonight. Did your plans change?'

'You could say that.' He moved closer, Dawud tucked in his arms.

'You look tense. Is something wrong?' She frowned. The way he looked at her began to make her nervous.

'A slight crisis, caused by the fact neither your security detail nor the palace staff had any idea where you were going this afternoon. You gave your bodyguards the slip.'

'I did no such thing! I told them I wanted time alone with Dawud. I didn't see them after that.'

Idris shook his head. 'You thought they'd return to the palace without you? That's more than their jobs are worth, or their honour. They withdrew to give you space but they couldn't let you walk off alone. You gave them the fright of their lives when they lost you in the covered bazaar.'

Arden scrambled to her feet, shock hitting.

'You told me Dawud and I were safe in Zahrat. Everyone was friendly in the markets, and you said yourself it would be a good thing for us to get about more with the people, rather than being surrounded by courtiers.'

Idris shut his eyes for a second and Arden knew he was gathering his patience. She hated this feeling that, again, she'd inadvertently done the wrong thing. Nor was she used to explaining her every move.

'Is it so wrong to want to spend time doing something normal?'

'Normal?' He looked as if he'd never heard the word.

Arden gestured wide. Even her choice of picnic spot was dictated by the fact royals didn't simply set themselves down to eat in public parks. Weeks ago Idris had shown her this little palace on its own rocky outcrop just beyond the city. It had been the dower residence of his grandmother and Arden loved its tranquillity and beauty. Today she hadn't been ready to return to the palace and, after just over three months in Zahrat, this was the only other private place she knew.

'Yes, normal. Doing a little shopping. Passing the time of day. Spending time with other mothers and children.'

It wasn't till she'd visited the playgroup that she'd realised how much she missed those small freedoms. She'd been invited in her role as Sheikha, but in reality it had been plain Arden, mother of an inquisitive, busy toddler, who'd chattered with the other mums. 'I need some freedom, Idris. You must understand that.'

With a sigh, Idris lowered Dawud to the ground

then wrapped his palm around the back of his neck as if easing an ache. It made her want to massage his knotted muscles, and wish she'd never even thought of a picnic.

Dawud plonked down at their feet and reached for some dried apricots.

'Idris?'

'I understand. You weren't born to this world. It takes a lot of adjustment. But next time let the staff know what you intend. You caused a security scare going off grid like that.' The corners of his mouth tucked down and he rolled his shoulders.

Seeing his tension, Arden felt a familiar wriggle of guilt in her belly. She got it every time she said the wrong thing at a royal event or broke some unwritten tradition.

'How much of a security scare?' Her eyes rounded. 'That helicopter?' At his nod she squeezed her eyes shut. Had they mobilised the army too? She felt about an inch tall. 'I'm so sorry. I didn't realise.'

Idris was right. She didn't understand all the rules. His life would have been easier if he'd married a real princess who knew how to behave and didn't disrupt the smooth workings of the royal machine.

Arden shook her head. She refused to go there again. She was doing her best.

'Hey.' An arm wrapped around her, tugging her against him. She opened her eyes to find herself fixed by his dark, velvety gaze. 'It's all right. There's no harm done.'

Her mouth crumpled in a travesty of a smile. 'I'm sure it's not but thanks for pretending. Just tell me, my bodyguards won't get into trouble, will they?'

He shook his head. 'Chastened but fine. Think of it as keeping them on their toes.' A sudden grin lit his face. 'You're good for them. They have no chance to get complacent.'

This time her smile felt real, but still distress lurked. She'd so enjoyed this afternoon. Hadn't dreamed it could hurt.

'What are you thinking?' His breath warmed her forehead as his arm slipped around her waist.

'That next time I want to go on a picnic I'll probably have three chefs and a dozen attendants with me. After filling out a security form detailing my intended movements down to the minute.'

'It's not that bad.' When she raised her eyebrows his lips twisted. 'Not *quite* that bad. And I'll see what I can do about making things easier. Starting right now.'

'Now?' Surely her little escape had ended.

'Now.' His voice deepened and a slow smile lightened his features. 'You've got me away from the office and I intend to make the most of it. I vote we play hooky together.'

Abruptly he sank to the ground, pulling her with him so she fell across his lap. She had an impression of midnight eyes and gleaming golden skin then his lips were on hers, not softly but with a pent-up hunger she recognised. Arden grabbed his shoulders, fire igniting instantly at her feminine core.

She was just going under for the third time when a strident voice piped up. 'Mama.' A little, warm body pushed against her, one sticky hand touching her cheek. 'Dawud kiss too.'

She heard Idris's chuckle, felt him shift to tug Dawud close and for one exquisite moment let herself believe in the perfection of the three of them together, like a real family.

Idris made the most of his unscheduled escape from royal duties, turning the afternoon into an idyllic family adventure exploring the tiny but lovely old palace. Tiny by Zahrati standards. It was still a mansion, filled with gorgeous furnishings and with an unrivalled view to the coast, the city and the mountains beyond.

With Dawud they investigated, admiring splendid mosaics, bedrooms and grand salons. The palace was furnished with beautiful antiques but somehow felt more like a sprawling home than a royal estate.

Evening came and with it a grander picnic than anything Arden had imagined. White coated servants from the Palace of Gold spread turquoise and scarlet rugs on the grass. Braziers were lit around

the garden, glowing and scented. The array of de
licious food was a feast for the senses.

Later the servants disappeared and Dawud
nanny carried him, sleeping, to the car for the dri
back to the citadel.

Finally alone, Idris insisted on feeding Arde
dessert with his own hands. Ripe peaches, burs
ing with rich juice, dark red grapes still with th
bloom of the vine on them and sweet oranges.

Then he licked up the spills where juice ha
dripped. She laughed, buoyed by the delight
this special time alone, by the hungry look in h
husband's eyes and the eager yet tender touch
his hands as he stripped her clothes away. It wa
no surprise when Idris carried her inside to fir
that one of the beds had been made up with fir
linen sheets scented with cinnamon and rose pe
als. Candles glowed around the room, turning
into a romantic bower.

'The honeymoon we never had,' Idris said whe
she exclaimed at the beauty of the scene. Then I
laid her on the bed and she stopped thinking abo
her surroundings.

Arden gasped for air, her lungs tight. Her bloo
pounded as bliss shuddered through her in afte
shocks so intense she thought they'd never end.

She didn't want them to end. Not when Idr
was there, above her, inside her, surrounding h
with his big body and powerful shoulders, qua

ing like her as his climax slowly faded. She felt the throb of his life force, the sensation that together they touched heaven, and she didn't want to let go.

She loved him coming apart in her arms, his weight hemming her in, his breath jagged in her ear, his formidable control shattered. In this they were equals and she revelled in it.

He groaned against her shoulder, sending fresh waves of pleasure juddering through her. Then Idris rolled onto his back, pulling her with him to sprawl naked across his steaming body.

Arden squinted one eye open, seeing the pink flush of dawn streaming in the open window. Soon Idris would get up to begin work.

But she didn't want to leave the Dower Palace. The spell of the place enveloped her. She wanted to hold Idris here, make him stay so she could enjoy the luxury of being alone with him, away from royal responsibilities. Here she'd felt not only happy but cherished.

Was she reading too much into last night's bliss? Into their sexual compatibility? Was she mistaking the afterglow of orgasm for a tenderness centred on mutual feeling?

'I was thinking,' he murmured, his lips moving against her hair, one arm wrapped around her waist.

'Hmm?'

'About another baby.'

Arden stilled, her finger poised where it had been stroking light circles across his ribs.

'A baby?'

'A brother or sister for Dawud. What do you think?' Did she imagine a thread of excitement in his voice? No. She'd been wrong. Idris sounded as calm as ever.

'You want another child?'

'Don't you?'

Yes. The answer slammed into her. She didn't need to think about it. Something deep down, something intrinsic to the woman she was, knew the answer as if she'd pondered it long and hard.

Arden blinked, stunned by the excitement she felt bubbling up. She'd got pregnant so young she hadn't really had time to think about having kids and since having Dawud she'd been too busy even to consider a relationship and another child.

'Arden?' Idris crooked a finger under her chin, lifting her face. He was propped up a little, his arm folded behind his head. The way he lay emphasised the impressive muscles of his arm and shoulder. Instantly heat drilled through her tight chest to her pelvis. Exhausted from sex and still she craved this man!

'Yes? I...' She refocused on his question. 'I don't know,' she prevaricated, for reasons she didn't understand. 'Why do you want another?'

Those jet eyebrows crunched together as if he

didn't like her question. Had he expected her to jump at the idea? That was intriguing.

'Don't you think a sibling would be good for Dawud?'

'Possibly.' Actually, she thought it would be wonderful but she reminded herself she owed it to her son and herself to do more than act impulsively. She'd done that when she fell for Idris years ago and it had turned her life on its head.

'Neither of us had siblings. We know how lonely that can be, especially when tragedy strikes.'

Grimly Arden nodded, her stomach cramping, not at the memory of those lonely childhood years bereft of family but at the idea of anything happening to Idris.

Horror filled her. A deep-down chill like the one she'd felt six months ago when for a few heart-numbing minutes she'd lost Dawud in a crowded shop.

She laid her palm flat on Idris's chest, feeling the steady thump of his heart, telling herself it was stupid to hypothesise about tragedy striking down Idris.

'Besides,' he went on, unaware of her fear, 'it sounds old-fashioned but it's a good way to ensure the security of the throne, and the nation, for the future. That's an important consideration too.'

'In case anything happens to Dawud?' Her voice was harsh.

Idris cupped a soothing palm around her bare shoulder. 'Nothing is going to happen to Dawud. But you never know—' he smiled in the way he knew made her melt '—our firstborn may want to go off and become an academic like my cousin, or a rock star. Having a brother to take the throne—'

'Or a sister,' she bit out, anger rising. As the law currently stood, only a male could inherit the throne. Unfair as she thought it, it wasn't that fuelling her temper. It was the notion she should have Idris's child to keep the throne safe and avoid political turmoil. They were talking about children! Children who deserved to be loved for themselves. Not pieces in some dynastic game!

'Or a sister.' Idris raised one eyebrow. 'Which would lead us to a discussion on exactly how many children we'd like to have.'

She recognised that lazy smile. It spoke of sexual promise. She had no complaints about making love with Idris. He made her feel not only satisfied but treasured. Which showed how skilled Idris was. To him having a child meant sex, which he clearly enjoyed. Enjoyed it enough to appear almost insatiable for her, a woman foisted on him by circumstance rather than personal preference.

But having a baby was about a lot more than that, as she knew too well.

'I'll think about it.' She pulled back, putting a little distance between them and watching his complacent smile slip. 'It's a lot to ask.'

His stare raked her. Clearly he hadn't expected that response. 'Of course.' Yet a frown rippled his broad brow and his grip on her shoulder tightened. 'There's plenty of time to think it over. Neither of us is going anywhere.'

Because he'd given his word.

Because he'd married her in front of thousands of witnesses.

Because he had no other choice but to stick with her.

Suddenly exhaustion filled her.

She hadn't married for love, other than the love of a mother for her child. She'd actually been enjoying her marriage to Idris, discovering as the months passed that their marriage suited her. *He* suited her. Even her life in Zahrat, though still challenging, brought satisfaction and a tentative sense of accomplishment. So why did the reminder that this was a purely practical union bring a bitter taint to her tongue?

Because your husband sees all this—you, your marriage, even your children—through the lens of practicality. Whereas for you...your heart is engaged.

Idris hauled her close, cupping the back of her head and drawing her against his chest. Automatically Arden fitted herself to him, one knee across his thigh, an arm round his waist.

But her mind raced, horrified by the stark truth of her discovery. That sudden, unbearable flash of insight had exploded her convenient belief that she could accept a loveless marriage.

Furtively she blinked back the haze of moisture misting her view of the dawn.

How had she deluded herself so long? It seemed impossible she'd never seen the truth before.

You didn't want the truth. You were wilfully blind because you knew the implications and didn't want to face them.

Arden bit her lip and tried not to panic, but it was almost impossible.

She'd congratulated herself on being reasonable and civilised, giving Dawud's father shared access. Accepting a sensible, convenient marriage though it meant living with a man she barely knew and embracing a whole new culture, giving up her safe, familiar world.

She'd even applauded the fact she could embark on a sexual relationship with the man she'd once loved and it wouldn't matter.

Of course it mattered.

Some sly part of herself must have realised the truth from the first. That it hadn't been so much of a sacrifice to marry him.

Because she was in love with Idris.

She had been all along. Only pride and pain had made her pretend she wasn't.

He was the only lover she'd ever had and, she realised with a hollow fear that threatened to engulf her, the only man she'd ever want.

* * *

Back at the Palace of Gold, Arden paced her sitting room, arms folded tight around her middle as if that could prevent the deep-seated ache inside.

Idris had left her with a bold kiss and a gleam in his eyes as soon as they returned from the Dower Palace. She'd clung to him, desperate to be held, though her brain said she needed to break free and decide what to do. For that she needed space and solitude.

First she'd cancelled her appointments for the day, surprising an understanding smile on one of the secretaries. Arden supposed all the palace staff knew she and Idris had spent an unscheduled belated honeymoon night.

Then she'd gone to Dawud, eager for the familiarity of his sturdy little frame and bright smile. She joined him in a game involving toy cars and a road map floor mat and lots of noise. But even as she smiled and crawled along, there was a terrifying blankness inside her where she fiercely shut out the hurt that would flood in if she let it.

Finally, when she felt calm enough to face what she must, she'd left Dawud with Misha and come here to her room. Stopping by the window she stared out beyond the city to the small Dower Palace.

She longed to recapture the magic of last evening. The thrill of being with Idris, not as a bride forced upon him by circumstance but as his lover.

The woman who loved him and for a few thoughtless hours had lived as carefree and content as if he loved her too.

The wall damming the dark pain cracked and despair poured out, making her clutch at the window frame with the force of that hurt.

Desperate, she told herself nothing had changed. Idris had never pretended to love her. He was decent and caring, dependable, honourable and, yes, charming. She loved his wry humour and he was great with Dawud. The pair were building a fantastic rapport.

It was she who'd changed. Or, if her suspicions were correct, not changed, but finally realised she'd been fooling herself. Because she loved Idris with all her being. Just as she'd loved Shakil all those years ago. Loved and lost.

Arden clawed the window frame and sank, a bundle of brittle bones, onto the window seat.

Loving and losing was a constant theme in her life.

First her parents. Then her foster parents. Then Shakil.

Now Idris.

No, she wouldn't lose him, not that way. He'd promised to stay with her, support her and do the right thing by Dawud. He'd do it, she knew he would. She knew him now, better than she had all that time ago. He saw this marriage as his duty and he'd stick at it no matter what.

There'd be no divorce. But Arden wasn't a naïve girl now. She knew a man like Idris would have sexual needs long after he lost interest in her. This honeymoon period, prompted she guessed by novelty and his desire for more children, would end soon enough.

What then? Arden had told him she didn't want to find out about his lovers. He hadn't demurred, simply agreed and moved on. At the time she'd been devastated at the idea of marrying a man already planning to be with other women.

That was before she realised she loved him.

How could she cope when he turned away and discreetly found with other women what he no longer wanted from her?

A tearing sound rent the air and she realised it was a groan of pain.

Idris would turn his back and she'd be left high and dry. Again.

Once more she'd got her hopes up. She hadn't consciously thought that one day her husband might come to love her but it had been there, a hidden nugget of hope, all this time.

She'd always craved love, stability, someone to value her as the most important person in their life. Every time hope had been snatched away.

Was that her fate? To seek love and always be disappointed?

She couldn't live like this, as merely a necessary wife. Idris cared about her but not enough.

Loving him when he felt only mild affection, seeing him turn to other women, would destroy her. She wouldn't let that happen. She would be strong, for herself and for Dawud. It was the way life had made her.

Arden got to her feet, grimacing at her creaky movements, as if the hoary fingers of age already claimed her. Slowly she straightened, her eyes fixed on the beautiful little palace beyond the city.

She had to find a way to survive this deal they'd made, do the best for Dawud, and for Idris, but keep her self-respect. And she had an inkling how she could do it.

This time she wouldn't be the one left behind.

CHAPTER THIRTEEN

A QUICK RAP on his study door made Idris look
up, his brain still grappling with the new draft of
the treaty.

Ashar stood in the doorway, his features so carefully blank that unease instantly ripped up Idris's
backbone. It reminded him of yesterday when his
aide had come to report that Arden was driving
out of town, destination unknown.

This was worse. He sensed it.

'Tell me.'

Not Arden. Not Dawud.

The ferocity of his fear for them paralysed him.

'They're both fine. Both well.' Ashar stepped
over the threshold, closing the door behind him,
and Idris sagged in his swivel chair, his fingers
grabbing the edge of the desk too tight. His heart
catapulted against his ribs, its rhythm sharp.

'But?' Idris tried to tell himself it was another
small misunderstanding. It couldn't be anything
major. Despite her doubts, Arden was increasingly
adept at dealing with courtiers and the public. As

for visiting VIPs, she charmed them with an ease that made him want to laugh. This was the woman his advisers had doubted could hold her own in public and she was proving his best asset with her unconventional, direct ways.

He wished he'd had her at his side when he'd first taken the role of Sheikh. The burdens would have been much lighter, and his life so much better.

'Tell me, Ashar.' His aide's silence was unnerving.

Idris watched him take a chair on the other side of the desk. 'The Sheikha and the little Prince are both at the Dower Palace.'

Idris let his pent-up breath surge out. For a moment he'd feared something terrible.

'Another picnic?' A smile curved his mouth. He'd toyed with the idea of shirking all his appointments today and spending time with his family. Amazing how much the idea appealed. He'd had to force himself out of Arden's arms and their bed in the little palace, telling himself this new treaty, and the meeting on improving infrastructure for remote provinces, were too vital to delay.

But he'd vowed to take Arden back there soon. Last night had felt like the honeymoon they'd never had. More, as if they'd found a new level of understanding. Their necessary marriage had blossomed in a way he'd never expected. She made him *happy*, he realised. Happy and proud. It was a revelation.

Ashar shook his head. He opened his mouth but didn't speak. Instead he cleared his throat.

Foreboding dimmed Idris's smile. 'Out with it, quickly.'

Ashar looked down at his hands. 'The Sheikha has co-opted several palace staff to help her refurbish the Dower Palace.'

'Refurbish?' Idris didn't know if he was more perplexed by the idea of it needing refurbishment or the fact Arden had directed staff to do anything. She was notoriously unwilling to issue orders, unused to having paid servants.

Ashar shrugged. 'Perhaps not refurbish. But open up the rooms ready to be lived in.' He paused, his gaze lifting to Idris. 'She gave the impression the order came from you.'

Ashar met his wary eyes. They both knew Idris had given no such order.

'Anything else?'

His secretary's expression flickered with something that might have been sympathy. 'I understand your wife and son's belongings have been packed up and moved out of the Palace of Gold.'

Idris slammed the door of his four-wheel drive and signalled his staff to remain here in the courtyard of the Dower Palace. Anger took him across the cobbled yard to the arch where ancient wooden doors, said to be as old as his family's rule on the throne of Zahrat, sat open.

A couple of strides took him to another, smaller courtyard and a maid, her arms full of bed linen. Her eyes rounded when she saw him and she stopped, curtseying.

'You're to leave here now and return to your usual duties.' His voice rasped out, harsh and unrecognisable. Like the fury he only just held in check. Fury that Arden would play such a game, trying to make a fool of him. 'Tell the other staff to stop what they're doing and get out immediately. Close the front doors behind you.'

She bobbed her head and scurried away, clasping the linen to her chest.

Idris stalked forward, through more doors, across the courtyard where just last night Arden had lain in his arms while he fed her sweet treats and seduced her into boneless compliance.

Of all the emotions that had rushed through him at Ashar's news, the strongest was hurt. Hurt that after all he and Arden had shared, after the sense of wordless understanding he'd woken to this morning, she should play such a trick. He couldn't believe she'd deliberately make him a laughing stock. Or that she was attempting some sort of blackmail, moving out to secure a better deal for herself.

When had he not given her what she desired?

When had he withheld his support? His riches?

When had he been anything but the best husband he could be? And in return he knew she'd strived to meet the demands of her new role.

So what was she playing at?

If she was unhappy she just had to say and he'd deal with the problem.

But this wasn't something she wanted him to fix. That was clear from the fact she'd moved out and taken Dawud.

This was a pre-emptive strike.

He'd trusted her! Let her become part of his life in ways he'd never imagined letting any woman, and she'd betrayed him.

He couldn't believe it. Or the excruciating ache in his heart.

Room after room passed. Some untouched, some bearing traces of recent change. Dustcovers removed. Mirrors sparkling. Mosaic floors glistening from scrubbing. He passed the room where they'd spent the night but it was deserted. Another room and there was a familiar white bed, tucked in a corner by the window. The mat he'd bought Dawud, a carpet road map for him to play on, lay beside it. Idris recognised the books and toys on top of a new dresser, and in the bed a tousled dark head, a small hand still grasping a teddy as Dawud slept.

Idris stopped, his heart skidding against his sternum as relief battered him. *Dawud was safe.*

He drew in a deep breath, then another, trying

to ease the hammering of his pulse as his gaze ate
up the sight of his boy.

Something, some infinitesimal sound made him
turn. Seconds later he was in the doorway of another bedroom. A white sheet snapped in the air
as it was flung across a bed. A bed much smaller
than the one he and Arden shared. Yet it was
Arden smoothing the crisp cotton down the mattress. Arden, not in her finery but wearing a simple
white sleeveless dress. Arden with her hair gleaming in the sunset glow coming from the window.

Idris stepped into the room, securing the door
behind him. The snick of the lock made her look
up, then her hand was at her throat, her face pale
as chalk.

'Idris! You scared me!'

He folded his arms across his chest, not both-
ering now to keep a lid on the ire that had burned
and bubbled since his aide's visit. Was Idris the last
in the royal compound to hear that his wife had
moved out, sneaking their son with her?

Arden's hand fell to her side and she backed a
step as if the sight of him frightened her. *Good!*

'I didn't expect to see you yet.'

Yet? That implied she *had* intended to see him.
He felt a trickle of relief. Till he wondered where
she'd planned to meet him. In the office of a divorce lawyer? No lawyer in the country would
take her on. He'd see to that.

'I suppose you're wondering what I'm doing?'

Her hands twisted together till she saw him notice and hauled them behind her back like a naughty schoolgirl. But this was no teenage prank.

'Why don't you say something?' Her voice was thin, as if stretched taut by emotion. Which was all wrong. She'd planned this deliberately, with cold calculation. *He* was the one feeling.

'I'm waiting for an explanation.'

'I…' Her hand climbed her throat again, fingers splaying nervously, till she blinked and dropped her arm. Her chin tilted. 'I'm moving out.'

Idris stared, watching her lips circle the words, hearing them resonate in his ears, and yet the sound didn't seem real. It was as if she spoke from a long distance, the words muffled by the skip of his pulse and the throbbing tension wrapping him so tight he felt his skin would split and bleed.

'Explain!'

'Dawud and I—' She gestured: a quick circular motion encompassing the room and, presumably, the one next door. 'We'll live here. It will work out better this way. I was going to tell you—'

'Really? And when were you going to impart this news?' His voice was barely above a growl, low, guttural and cold as her frigid English heart. 'Before or after the whole city heard about it?'

Her eyes widened and her mouth sagged. 'No, I—'

'No, you weren't going to tell me after all? You

were going to let me find out for myself? Just as, in fact, I did?'

Fury rose to towering levels. He paced the room, planting himself between Arden and the door. She'd betrayed him, made a fool of him, stolen his son. He'd woken this morning to a sense of peace and promise unlike any he'd ever known. He'd looked forward to building a family with her and all the time she'd planned to leave.

He'd never known such pain as that tearing at his vitals. Only years of warrior training kept him upright.

If she thought he'd permit her to get away with this she was incredibly naïve.

Arden looked up into hard, fathomless eyes. She didn't recognise them. Didn't recognise the man before her. This wasn't the bronzed warrior prince she'd come to love. This was a stranger. As he uncrossed his arms and flexed his fingers she shivered.

She told herself to buck up. She'd known this wouldn't be easy. But if she was to preserve her sanity and her self-respect it had to be done.

'Why don't we go somewhere more comfortable and sit down to discuss this?' She felt trapped by his forceful presence, literally cornered.

'Stop delaying.' He widened his stance and re-crossed his arms over his powerful chest, reinforcing that potent male power battering her shredded nerves.

How was she supposed to fight him when part of her wanted to nestle against that broad shoulder and accept what he offered her, even though it wasn't enough?

Arden swallowed a tangle of emotion and forced herself to meet his glare.

'This marriage isn't working for me. I had my doubts from the start, you know that, and...' She gestured vaguely. 'Well, it turns out I was right.'

'In what way isn't it working?' His face was so flinty, his expression so fixed, his lips barely moved.

'I don't feel...' *loved.* She couldn't admit that. 'You must understand.' Another quick wave of her hand. 'Zahrat, living in a palace, marriage to a sheikh; it's all a far cry from what I'm used to. And what I'm comfortable with.'

Was it possible that his thinned lips tightened even further?

'I don't feel able to continue like I have been, so I've come up with a compromise.'

'This doesn't look like compromise to me,' he snarled. 'This looks like desertion.'

Arden jammed her hands onto her hips, summoning anger to block out the pain in her heart. 'Desertion would be me taking Dawud on the next flight out of here and filing for divorce.' Her breath came so fast she couldn't keep going.

She heaved in more air and dredged up some words before he interrupted. 'Instead I propose to live here with Dawud. Close enough that you can still see him daily. He can go to the Palace of Gold to visit you or you could come here.' She paused. Having Idris here in what would be her sanctuary would just prolong her heartache. But what alternative could she offer?

Idris opened his mouth and she raised a hand to stop him. 'Just hear me out.' She snagged another quick breath. 'This way you have the marriage you needed and the heir but without the encumbrance of…me. You know I'm not good at the whole royal thing. Everyone will understand the split. I told the staff it was your order that I move here. People will think *you've* set me aside, and they won't be surprised because everyone knows I'm an embarrassment.' Heat crept up her cheeks at the memory of so many public blunders.

But in the scale of things those mistakes meant nothing. Not compared to walking away from the man she loved. Dully she wondered how long it would be before the hurt started to ease. Or if it ever would.

'I won't embarrass you if I'm living here, out of the public eye. And you'll be free to take lovers without worrying about me being on the premises.' Something within her collapsed, crumpling at the thought, but she kept her chin up. 'It's the best solution.'

Except she didn't believe it for a moment. Living in Zahrat, so close to Idris, would be torment. Yet for Dawud's sake she'd endure it.

Idris's gaze bored into hers. 'This is the second time you've mentioned my lovers. You seem inordinately interested in them.' Something flickered in that enigmatic dark stare. 'Why is that? Are you intending to vet them yourself to see they're not a negative influence on our son when they meet?'

'You wouldn't do that! You promised to be discreet and not flaunt them in front of Dawud.' Fury rose, a fiery column, scorching her from the inside. She actually took a step closer till she read the predatory stillness in Idris's big frame, the intensity of his haughty glare, and realised he was deliberately taunting her.

That casual cruelty punctured her indignation, leaving her empty and fragile. She swayed, praying for the strength to see this through.

'It's time to admit it's not working and accept a sensible compromise. You've done everything that could be expected of you, Idris. You've married me and legitimised Dawud. You've upheld your honour.'

Idris stared at her. A nervous, defiant woman who looked like the beautiful wife he'd taken to bed last night but couldn't be. His wife had spent the evening sighing her pleasure while setting out to please him more successfully than any other woman ever had.

Then, as usual, she'd curled confidingly close. He'd grown used to her snuggling against him as if, even in sleep, she needed physical intimacy to settle.

He'd grown used to greeting the dawn making love to her. More often than not sharing a bath or shower with her. He'd even become accustomed to chatting with her after formal events, sharing observations and insights, always fascinated by the different perspective she provided. And breakfasting with her and Dawud, enjoying a growing understanding and shared purpose in caring for their boy. He'd been proud of her progress in dealing with state occasions, and her surprising aptitude at his language. He'd laughed with her over things he'd never been able to share with others and found increasing pleasure in relaxing with her.

Over the past months she'd become more than a convenient bride. She'd become his *wife*.

How had it all gone wrong?

Why had she done this?

Idris stepped closer, watching with mingled satisfaction and pain as she shrank against the wall.

'Honour! You talk to me of honour? As if that's all this marriage is about?' He was so incensed he had to work to keep his voice low enough that it didn't disturb Dawud in the next room. Fire ran in his veins, a white-hot incendiary burn that ate him up from the inside, devouring him. Or perhaps that was the anguish he was trying not to think about.

'What about *us*, Arden? You and me? And Dawud?' He leaned over her and her head tilted back against the wall. But she didn't look scared any more. She looked tired, and that tore at him.

After what she'd done, and the way she'd insulted him, he felt *concerned* for her?

'As you say,' she said softly, 'this marriage is about you and me and our son. I think it best for Dawud not to grow up watching our marriage disintegrate. Better to make an amicable break now and come to a compromise that allows him to grow up with both of us.'

Compromise. There was that word again. Idris had never hated it so much.

'You're lying. Whatever is behind your actions, this isn't about Dawud. This—' a sharp gesture encompassed the half-made bed and his errant wife '—is about you and me.'

Instinct drove that observation and he saw it confirmed when her eyelids fluttered and her gaze skated sideways, as if she were scared he'd read the truth in her expression.

What *was* the truth? She'd hurt him as surely as if she'd taken his grandfather's ceremonial sword and sliced Idris right through the chest. He'd never experienced anything like this pain he was helpless to understand or control. It made him even more determined.

Another step took him into her space. Her chin tipped high to keep him in her sights. He sensed her fight or flight response in her sharp, tremulous breaths and her air of expectation.

Just let her try to flee. He'd enjoy stopping her.

'What could it be, I wonder?' He thought over her explanation.

'All that about being an embarrassment to me is whitewash. You don't embarrass me and you never have. You know that. I'm *proud* of the way you've adapted. You've got a gift for putting people at their ease, a gift for making them feel welcome. You like people, you're interested in them and that shows.'

Her eyes grew wide. 'But I—'

'No buts. You know it's true. Don't I tell you time and again how wonderful you are? How quickly you've mastered your royal duties? You've already won the hearts of half the schoolchildren in the country and their parents. That only leaves fifty per cent to go.'

Where he found levity from Idris didn't know, but the idea of Arden hiding like some shameful secret was totally absurd.

Her reasons for moving out didn't make sense.

'Then there's the question of my lovers.' She

flinched then schooled her expression into immobility. His hunter's instinct sharpened.

She cared about him having women?

Of course she cared. He'd be outraged if she didn't.

The idea of Arden and his cousin as lovers had unearthed previously unknown violent instincts in Idris, till she'd convinced him there'd been no man in her life for four years.

No man in her life but himself.

His thoughts slowed to a familiar, all-consuming satisfaction. Idris was her only lover and he intended it to stay that way. He couldn't countenance the idea of Arden with any other man. Ever.

Sudden heat bloomed in his chest as realisation smacked him.

He rocked back on his feet, actually taking a half step away as knowledge smote him.

'My lovers,' he repeated slowly, his brain, *finally*, catching up with instinct. 'You don't want to meet my lovers.'

The voice wasn't his. It was hoarse, thick and dull, stunned by what he'd blithely never considered before.

Had he really been so blind?

His heart hammered against his ribs and his breath came in sharp snatches, dragged into lungs that felt too small to cope with the enormity of the knowledge battering him.

'You promised. You agreed not to flaunt them

so Dawud or I would see them.' She glared, hands on her hips, her bottom lip jutting belligerently. In her white silk dress, with her hair in gilded waves around her shoulders and her aquamarine eyes dazzling like gems, she was stunning.

How could he want another woman when he had Arden?

He shook his head, blinking at the patent absurdity of it.

She stepped forward, prodding his chest. 'A man of *honour* wouldn't go back on his word.'

Idris clapped his hand over hers, pressing it against his racing heart. He saw her still, her eyes widen from slits of anger to pools of shimmering surprise.

'Feel that?' His voice was a raw rasp. 'You do that to me, Arden.' As he said it Idris felt the power of it fill him like a shaft of sunshine streaming all the way to the bottom of an abandoned, empty well.

Except he didn't feel empty now. He felt filled to the brim with fierce, choking, glorious feeling.

She tugged at her hand, her mouth turning down, her brow knotted. 'You're angry at the inconvenience I'm causing. That's all.'

'Not angry. Furious. I was furious. But I'm not now.'

Yet his heart rate didn't ease. His temper might have dried up but what he felt now was simultaneously the most amazing, frightening thing he'd ever experienced.

He swallowed hard, his Adam's apple bobbing painfully.

'I don't care, Idris. I just want you to let me go.' Arden's voice rose in a wailing sob that cut him to the bone. Her pain was his, tenfold.

He lifted his other hand and stroked the hair from her cheek, marvelling again at the softness of her skin. He closed his eyes, trying to save this moment of absolute awareness, inhaling her light orange blossom fragrance.

'There will be no other women.'

Finally she stopped trying to free herself. 'Pardon?'

'There won't be any other women for me. I never intended to take another lover.'

'But you agreed——'

His eyes snapped open and he looked down into her stunned face. 'I agreed never to flaunt a lover. I never said there would actually *be* any lovers.' He paused, amazed at how slow-witted he'd been. He'd never questioned why that was. 'I knew even then that I'd want no one else. I haven't since I met you again.'

Her mouth tightened. 'You're saying that because you think it will make me change my mind. But it won't. It's nothing to me if you have a whole harem of lovers.'

'Isn't it?' He cupped her cheek. 'You may not care but I would. I just couldn't do it.'

He stared into her grumpy, set features and told himself he owed her the truth, even if by some ill-omened fate he was wrong about Arden's feelings for him. His pulse sprinted like a mad thing and fear tightened his belly.

'Aren't you going to ask me why I couldn't take a lover?'

She blinked then looked away. He felt her tremble and her pain made his chest seize. 'Don't do this, Idris. I don't think I—'

'I couldn't take another woman into my bed because there's only one woman I'll ever want, in my bed and in my life. That's you, Arden. I love you, *habibti*. I have from the start, though I was too slow to see it. I felt it. I hated believing there'd been other men in your life. I hated feeling that you didn't need me or want me. That's one of the reasons I acted so quickly to secure you, before you could run off again.'

'I never ran anywhere.' Her eyes were round as saucers and her tremor intensified till she shook all over.

'It felt like it.' Now, in retrospect, he realised that was exactly how it had been. 'I deserted you because I had to face my responsibilities, my *duty*.' His mouth twisted. 'But it seemed like you'd run away with my heart. I never felt for any woman what I felt for you. Not in all the years we were apart.' He shook his head. 'Why do you think I made a beeline for your house the morning after the reception? I *had* to see you again, had to be with you, even though it was total insanity if I really planned to marry someone else.'

'Idris?' Arden's voice was a tremulous whisper, her mouth working. 'Please. Are you just saying this because—?'

'I'm saying it because it's true, Arden. I love you. You make me feel whole.' He fell to his knees before her, ignoring generations of royal pride, knowing only that he *had* to make her believe. He gathered her hands in his.

'I didn't think it possible. The men in my family never lose their hearts. All except King Dawud, my grandfather, who adored my grandmother till his dying day.' Idris pressed her hands, willing her to believe. 'That's my excuse for not realising how I felt about you. It didn't even occur to me that the jealousy and lust, the pride and admiration, the liking, were all part of love.'

He lifted first one of her hands, then the other, pressing kisses to each. 'I love you, Arden, with all my heart. With all that I am. On my honour, on the honour of my family and the memory of my grandfather, it's true.' He paused, emotions surging so high speech was difficult.

'But if you don't believe me yet, don't worry, you will. I intend to convince you every day for the rest of our lives.'

If she let him.

Tears glistened in her eyes and his heart cramped. Dismay filled him and dread that perhaps he'd been wrong to imagine she cared for him.

But before he could conjure a protest she'd sunk to her knees before him, her hands gripping his strongly.

Heart in mouth, he watched her raise his hand, then press her delicate lips to it. A ripple ran up his arm, across his shoulder to splinter to spread through his body. Slowly she kissed his other hand and his heart sang.

'I love you, Idris.' Those stunning eyes, washed, he realised, with tears of happiness, were the most beautiful in the whole world. 'I loved you in Santorini. I even loved you in the years we were apart though I told myself it wasn't so.' Her mouth curved in a secretive smile that melted his soul. 'I'll always love you.'

A huge sigh escaped him, shuddering out the pent-up breath he'd held too long. His whole being felt renewed, stronger, better. 'Then we're perfectly matched. For I will love you till the last breath in my body, and beyond.'

He watched the stars shine in her eyes, the sun rise in her smile and knew he'd come home.

'I have a suggestion.'

Her gaze slid to the bed beside them and he laughed, the sound of pure joy ringing around them. 'Soon, Arden.' Already he was strung taut and eager for her. 'But I wanted to suggest we move in here together, you, me and Dawud.'

'Really? But you need to be at the Palace of Gold. All your official responsibilities...'

'*Our* official responsibilities,' he amended. 'I propose that during the week we stay there, and do what's expected of a royal sheikh and sheikha. And on weekends we live here, out of the limelight, just being a family.'

'You could do that? Really?'

'*We* can do it. With some planning I don't see why not. In fact, I insist.'

Her smile said everything he could have wanted as he pulled her to him.

'It sounds just perfect.' Whatever else she intended to say was lost against his lips as he bestowed the first kiss of the rest of their lives. A kiss of love, offered and received. A kiss of promise.

* * * * *

If you enjoyed this story,
check out these other
great reads from Annie West
THE FLAW IN RAFFAELE'S REVENGE
A VOW TO SECURE HIS LEGACY
SEDUCING HIS ENEMY'S DAUGHTER
Available now!

And don't miss these other
SECRET HEIRS OF BILLIONAIRES
themed stories
DEMETRIOU DEMANDS HIS CHILD
by Kate Hewitt
THE SECRET TO MARRYING MARCHESI
by Amanda Cinelli
Available now!

LARGER-PRINT BOOKS!
GET 2 FREE LARGER-PRINT NOVELS PLUS
2 FREE GIFTS!

⊕ HARLEQUIN®

INTRIGUE
BREATHTAKING ROMANTIC SUSPENSE

YES! Please send me 2 FREE LARGER-PRINT Harlequin® Intrigue novels and my 2 FREE gifts (gifts are worth about $10). After receiving them, if I don't wish to receive any more books, I can return the shipping statement marked "cancel." If I don't cancel, I will receive 6 brand-new novels every month and be billed just $5.49 per book in the U.S. or $6.24 per book in Canada. That's a saving of at least 11% off the cover price! It's quite a bargain! Shipping and handling is just 50¢ per book in the U.S. and 75¢ per book in Canada.* I understand that accepting the 2 free books and gifts places me under no obligation to buy anything. I can always return a shipment and cancel at any time. Even if I never buy another book, the two free books and gifts are mine to keep forever.

199/399 HDN GHWN

Name _____
(PLEASE PRINT)

Address _____ Apt. #

City _____ State/Prov. _____ Zip/Postal Code

Signature (if under 18, a parent or guardian must sign)

Mail to the _____ 867 _____ A 5X3

Call _____ oks _____ ?

_____ ice.com.

* Terms and pr _____ include applicable taxes. Sales ta _____ applicable taxes. Offer not valid _____ current subscri _____ hold. Not valid for approval. Credi _____ s subject to credit outstanding bala _____ offset by any other Offer available v _____ eeks for delivery.

Your Privacy— _____ ur privacy. Our Privacy Policy i _____ n request from the Reader Ser _____

We make a portio _____ we believe may _____ at offer products parties, or if you _____ name with third us at www.Read _____ ces, please visit Preference Service, P.O. Box 9062, Buffalo, NY 14240-9062. Include your complete name and address.

HILP15